A Candlelight Ecstasy Romance ®

"YOU'D MARRY KERRY, KNOWING THAT YOU WANT TO GO TO BED WITH ME RIGHT NOW?"

"If I were entertaining the idea of going to bed with another man," she said with a cool smile, "I wouldn't be considering marriage to Kerry. But you can't know for sure that I want to go to bed with you."

He smiled, lifting his glass to his lips. "You're right. I can't know for sure. But I've got this . . . gut feeling."

"Just a gut feeling?" she asked with a laugh.

"Well, maybe a little *more* than a gut feeling, my dear." He enjoyed watching the deep flush that colored her face. "No comeback?" His breath warmed her as his lips softly nipped her skin.

She shivered, her breathing shallow and light. "I have, but I'll save it for later."

A CANDLELIGHT ECSTASY ROMANCE ®

BENEATH THE WILLOW TREE

Emma Bennett

A CANDLELIGHT ECSTASY ROMANCE ®

Published by
Dell Publishing Co., Inc.
1 Dag Hammarskjold Plaza
New York, New York 10017

Dell ® TM 681510, Dell Publishing Co., Inc.

Candlelight Ecstasy Romance®, 1,203,540, is a registered
trademark of Dell Publishing Co., Inc.
New York, New York.

ISBN: 0-440-10443-2

Printed in the United States of America
First printing—August 1983

To Our Readers:

We have been delighted with your enthusiastic response to Candlelight Ecstasy Romances®, and we thank you for the interest you have shown in this exciting series.

In the upcoming months we will continue to present the distinctive sensuous love stories you have come to expect only from Ecstasy. We look forward to bringing you many more books from your favorite authors and also the very finest work from new authors of contemporary romantic fiction.

As always, we are striving to present the unique, absorbing love stories that you enjoy most—books that are more than ordinary romance.

Your suggestions and comments are always welcome. Please write to us at the address below.

Sincerely,

The Editors
Candlelight Romances
1 Dag Hammarskjold Plaza
New York, New York 10017

CHAPTER ONE

Neal Freeman, clad in jeans and a soft cotton shirt, walked to her pickup truck, opened the door, and laid her medical bag on the seat. Before she swung herself in, however, she let her eyes run across the beauty of the Golden Cam, her gaze lingering wistfully on the rambling stone ranch house. She took off her hat and ran her fingers through her damp black curls. She'd forgotten how hot summers could be in the hill country.

She tucked the hat on her head, adjusted the brim, and caught the frame of the truck to lever herself in. Just as her booted foot hit the floorboard, she heard the arrival of another car. Wiggling comfortably into position on the leather seat, she curiously turned to look out the opened window of the truck. A Mercedes pulled alongside her, grinding to a halt in front of the house. Trying to look away, yet compelled by some inner curiosity which proved stronger than reason, she stared down at the man who drove the car.

Edric Cameron!

The words softly slipped past her lips, bringing vividly to life all those memories that had lain dormant—not forgotten but dormant—for so many years. Quickly she leaned forward, turned the key, and tapped the accelerator until the engine sputtered to life. Looking over her shoulder, but not really seeing the road, she began to back out.

The man had gotten out of the car, and most of his attention was directed to the task of getting his suit jacket and luggage from the back seat. As the cab of the truck reached eye level, though, he spared the driver a quick glance. He didn't recognize either the truck or the driver. But as his tawny eyes raked over the woman's face, he decided that he would certainly like to know her better. He was a man who thoroughly enjoyed women.

Neal's first impression was confirmed. Edric Cameron hadn't changed that much! His tall form was still sinewy and tough, even though it was clothed in a soft and expensive-looking outfit, a white shirt and brown slacks. His hair was styled differently, but it was still sable-black, thick and straight, with that errant lock falling across his forehead. His sun-bronzed face, the image safely locked in her memory, had changed little through the years.

He hoisted the suitcase in the air and moved around the hood of his car, still gazing with interest at the woman. Like her, he stared, and he had that flash of recognition. But he couldn't place her immediately. Short, curly black hair. He preferred long hair. The face, however, was familiar. No makeup, he noticed. Just a smooth healthy sheen. Those blue . . . He mentally stopped. No, he thought, moving closer to the truck, squinting, studying her more closely. Those eyes are not just blue. They're the color of bluebonnets. Color of bluebonnets, he repeated.

"Wait a minute!" He didn't know that he had thought the command, much less yelled it.

He dropped the suitcase to the ground, threw his jacket on the hood of his car, and walked to the truck, which had stopped moving. Bluebonnets! Only one woman he'd ever known had eyes that color. He moved to the side of the truck; his hands clasped the metal frame of the opened window.

10

"Neal?" His words were a hesitant whisper. "Neal Freeman?"

"Me," she replied easily, her blue-violet eyes roving over his face, a smile gently curving the corners of her mouth.

"What are you doing way out here at the Golden Cam?" His eyes never left her face, raking over each feature again and again.

Neal opened her mouth to speak, but Duncan Marsh, Edric's manager, walked up. His weather-beaten face was creased in a big smile and was covered with perspiration. He pulled a large red and black bandanna from his hip pocket and swiped at his face a time or two.

"Howdy, Ed," he greeted the younger man. "Been mighty hot today, and we been out in the pasture with the buffaloes." He stepped closer to Neal's truck, stuffing the kerchief into the back pocket.

Edric turned to smile at Duncan, the only person in the world whom he allowed to call him Ed. "Sorry, I couldn't get here any sooner, but you know how those meetings are."

Duncan nodded. "Figured it would be a while before you could get here, so I took matters into my own hands." He shoved his sweat-stained hat back on his forehead before he lowered his hands, letting them rest on his hips.

Edric lifted those thick black brows. "Under control?"

Again Duncan nodded.

"What'd Sam say?" Concern thickly laced Edric's words together.

A mischievous grin replaced Duncan's smile. "Didn't say nothing."

Perplexity fleeted across Edric's face, clouding his eyes. "That's not like Sam."

Duncan pursed his lips for a second, then said, "Well, as a matter of fact, Eddy—"

11

Neal grinned as Edric grimaced. Remembering his aversion to nicknames, she was mildly surprised when Edric said nothing.

"—Sam didn't exactly come to look at the critters," Duncan continued.

When Neal laughed quietly, Edric darted a suspicious glance at her; then his eyes flicked back to the older man, who stood quite offhandedly in front of the truck, kicking pebbles at his feet.

"What makes you think everything is under control?" Edric's question was one extended sigh. He knew they were playing a game, Duncan's game, and he also knew he had no alternative but to play along.

Duncan chuckled, thoroughly enjoying his joke and Edric's irritation. He rubbed his chin. "Now, Eddy, don't go getting yourself so worked up."

Edric's eyes narrowed. "Duncan!" The ejaculation was a mixture of controlled anger and frustration. As much as he loved the older man, he could throttle him when he was in one of these moods.

Duncan again ran his hand across his chin. "The vet's been here," he slowly admitted, "but it wasn't Sam." The faded blue eyes moved from Edric's face to Neal's.

Edric turned. "You! You're the vet!" The exclamation hovered between them.

"The same," Neal replied, that easy smile lingering on her lips, her eyes humorously resting on the masculine face in front of her.

Edric's lips, which had thinned into a line of concern and anxiety, now relaxed, and their sensual fullness parted into a smile, a smile that radiated from his soul. His eyes, his unforgettable golden topaz eyes, lighted up in a warm greeting also. Completely turning his back to Duncan, he moved closer to the truck.

Duncan, chuckling softly to himself, walked in the direction of the house. It'd been a mighty long time since that little lady had been here, and he was going to let them have their privacy. He certainly wanted Edric to have a chance to get to know her again. Heck, poor Edric had been through hell the past seven years.

Edric's father had died less than a year after his mother's fatal heart attack, and Edric had been racked with grief for months. And that Alexa woman had been hanging around Edric at the right time. She was conveniently available just when the young man had needed a shoulder to cry on. What a performance, Duncan recalled. She could have won an Academy Award, that one. Then, before anyone knew what had happened, Edric married her.

And she was nothing but a bitch, Duncan thought. All she wanted was to change him and to get her hands on his money. She had hated the ranch and all that it meant to Edric. Sell, she kept insisting. Get rid of it. Let's move to the city. For three years Edric had tried; then he gave up and didn't care. And for the past three years since the divorce he'd thrown himself into the ranch.

Time he found a good woman, Duncan figured, and he wasn't ashamed of his Cupid playing. Neal would be good for Edric. She loved the land as he did. And there'd been the time when that little lady had been mighty fond of Edric. Yes, sir, he thought, disappearing into the house, them buffaloes getting sick was about the best thing that had happened for quite a spell around the Golden Cam.

As Duncan ambled into the house, Edric stood by the truck, looking at Neal. He should have known, he thought. He should have! But she'd matured. Her hair was short now instead of long. Her lips! God, he could still taste the honeyed sweetness of them. Those eyes! He could as easily lose himself in their beauty today as he had

. . . Had it been that long? He counted the years. Yes, it had been that long.

Neal could almost see the memories as they one by one paraded through Edric's mind, and he deliberately lifted the curtain from his eyes so she could view them, too. The painful ones he adroitly sidestepped, but the others he put in the limelight, letting the telltale desire lap in tiny flames at the bottom of the golden brown spheres. A younger Neal would have responded to his message, but the mature Neal reacted passively to that look, avoiding the intimacy his gaze invited, denying the unspoken accusation that she too had never forgotten all she and Edric had once shared.

"Hello, Neal." The vibrant tones stirred the strings of cherished memories. "Welcome back home. Welcome to the Golden Cam."

"Hello, Edric." She loved the taste of his name in her mouth. She loved the feel of it on her tongue and her lips. How natural it felt! How right it was! How natural it sounded to her ears!

She was surprised at how quickly the years could slip away. As if it were tidal wave in proportion, the anguish of her humiliation washed over her anew, leaving her again drenched in sorrow. Poignantly she remembered all the pain and grief of his rejection.

Yet, at the same time, her body remembered the exquisite delight of his touch, and it wanted to rebel against the strict commands of her mind. Not understanding reason, her body wanted his touch; it wanted once again to experience his expressions of love.

But reason reigned supreme for the moment. Neal forced herself to remain in her relaxed pose, and she demanded that her body convey a show of casualness.

For endless seconds Edric and Neal looked at each other, lost in time, lost in place, expressionless. They tuned out the lazy sounds of nature around them, they

14

forgot all about Duncan, and they stared, only their eyes moving as each surveyed the face of the other. Though there was no physical movement, Neal felt as if Edric had just this moment traced her face with his fingertips, so intense was his visual caress.

The moment his hand reached up, his fingers coming close but not quite touching the short curls that bunched in organized disarray around her face, the muscles around her heart constricted. For an instant she wondered if she'd ever breathe again.

"You've cut your hair." No censure. Maybe disappointment. More than likely just an observation.

Involuntary brain impulses forced the breath into her lungs, through her body, and she gulped. She swallowed convulsively, apprehension and anxiety tied in a knot that lodged in her throat. She nodded.

Edric continued to stare into her face, searching for the girl he'd known so long ago. No longer a youngster. She'd matured, he thought, his hand dropping from her hair to cling to the door handle. She'd probably changed, too, he surmised, his fingers closing over the chrome fixture, gently squeezing and pulling at the same time, so that the door was opened just a crack. But those eyes were the same, large and lucent. Would they talk to him again? he wondered. Would they murmur sweet endearments to him now? Or were they as cold and unfeeling as they looked? He opened the door further.

"Won't you come in and visit for a spell?" he asked.

The smile never left Neal's face, but she shook her head. "I wish I could," she explained, "but I've got to head back to town." Her hand caught the door, and she pulled it toward herself in an effort to close it.

Edric didn't turn it loose, though; he didn't want her to leave. "Since I'm here, don't you think we ought to discuss

15

your diagnosis of the buffaloes? I am concerned, you know. Sam usually . . ."

"I've already talked with Duncan," she returned evenly, slightly amused, slightly disconcerted by his cool deliberation, his overt method of keeping her at the ranch.

Even though she had known there was a possibility of a confrontation with Edric when Duncan had called, she had had no choice but to come. You could have referred Duncan to another vet, to one closer to the ranch, she thought self-accusingly. No, I couldn't. Sam wouldn't have stood for that. He's been taking care of the Golden Cam stock for as long as I can remember and probably for as long as he can remember. Once at the ranch, however, she found that she wanted to stay, if for no other reason than curiosity. She wondered if the place had changed. She wondered if Edric had changed. Still, she wouldn't allow herself to get too entangled with him again. She hadn't fully recovered from her last involvement with Edric Cameron.

Edric couldn't read her thoughts, but he sensed her hesitation. He felt her indecision, so he pressed his advantage.

"Duncan isn't me, Dr. Freeman."

"No," she slowly drawled, her eyes again moving over his face, coming to rest on those expressive brown eyes. "Duncan isn't you." There will never be another you, Edric Cameron. Then she saw the twinkle in his eyes and knew that once again she had become a victim of their charm. Mentally shaking herself, she suddenly chuckled. "Thank God for small favors. What would the world do with two of you on the loose?"

"Thank you, too," Edric returned dryly before he asked, "Well, are you coming in or not?" His eyes met hers squarely, holding them, refusing to let her leave, trying to impress his will on her.

16

He remembered Neal Freeman as a fantastic lover, fiery and passionate. What would she be like now? he wondered. Matured. Emotionally and physically. His eyes raked over the breasts that were clearly defined in the faded cotton shirt. His eyes rested on the fullness, remembering the creamy smoothness of her skin. His glowing eyes traveled lower, scanning the trim hips and the slender legs. Then the tawny orbs lifted, and Neal was left in no doubt about his thoughts and feelings.

His gaze was like a match which lit the dormant passions in her body, kindling them to life again. And in answer to the silent command they began to flame. Molten desire, hot, fluid, raced through her bones and her veins, carrying the heated message to every cell in her body, and would have blazed a path to her eyes to burn brightly for Edric to see. Just in time the remembered pain and humiliation surfaced, acting like a barrier to shield those emotions from him. But it didn't stop her from feeling them, from wanting to move to him and to fling herself into his arms.

Not certain of what she would do, Edric exerted all his persuasive charm. "For old times' sake, Neal."

Neal hadn't forgotten the strong pull of this man's charm. Her body wanted to obey Edric's summons, but she couldn't. She had to withstand these emotions, or she couldn't save herself. Breaking eye contact, she looked at the stone fence in front of her. She couldn't respect herself if she let Edric lead her on another one of those romantic wild-goose chases.

"Sorry," she said, "not today."

She revved the engine, which had been idling.

"How about one drink?" he continued, never raising his voice, his eyes never leaving her face. "I'd bet you're pretty thirsty."

Again she shook her head. "Sorry, but I don't drink

17

when I'm working." Although her answer was the truth, in this instance it sounded rather juvenile.

Edric responded by laughing at her, a deep, rumbling sound. When he could finally speak, he said, "Not even a Coke or a glass of iced tea?" His eyes twinkled, sparkling in the afternoon sunlight.

Neal's quiet refusal was lost in the thunderous bellowing from the house.

"Y'all come on in. Molly's got a pitcher of her fresh lemonade fixed. She thought you'd be mighty thirsty, Neal, after working on them critters all afternoon."

Neal looked from Duncan to Edric. How could she refuse now? Molly had prepared that lemonade just for her, she thought. But it wouldn't go to waste. She smiled. If she remembered correctly, Duncan loved his wife's lemonade and could quaff most of it in one sitting. She shook her head again, reaching a second time for the door.

"Sorry," she called to Duncan, "but I've got to get going. Until Sam's over the flu, I've got my hands full."

"Neal Freeman!" The female voice sailed across the lawn, and the command in the two words was evident to all who heard. Neal turned her face and saw the tall, slender form of Molly Marsh as she pushed past Duncan through the door and across the lawn.

"You're not about to leave here until you have some lemonade and until we talk awhile." At the truck now, she glared at Neal. "I made it especially for you." Her tone allowed no argument, but she did smile. "I made some tea cakes, too."

Duncan, who had slowly meandered across the yard after Molly, said, "Reckon you'll be staying, Neal. Nobody, including me and Edric, disobeys Molly."

Neal looked at the circle of faces around her, and she began to laugh softly with them. She shrugged, admitting

18

defeat. A glass of cold lemonade sounded too good to miss. She pushed the gear into park and turned off the ignition.

As she turned in the seat, Edric stepped closer and clasped her waist with both his hands, swinging her clear of the truck. When he placed her feet on the ground, he whispered in her ear. "I'll bet you thought I'd forgotten that, didn't you?" The memory, the touch, the whisper—all were designed to fray her emotions, and they succeeded.

Neal laughed, but she wanted to cry. How many years had she been trying to forget? But she couldn't; she couldn't forget anything about Edric, not even the hurt and the pain. Even now she had to quell the riotous feelings that were running wildly through her veins. She could hardly hear the teasing comments of Molly and Duncan as they stepped away from the truck.

"Did you think I'd forgotten?" Edric repeated, his eyes searching hers, seeking a sign of her awakening passion.

"To tell the truth," she said, prevaricating, "I hadn't thought much about it one way or the other." Her confession sounded genuine; there was a ring of truth to it. "And," she continued, gently pushing out of Edric's arms, "it happened too many years ago for me to want to remember."

Edric continued to look at her while Molly and Duncan led the procession to the house. Molly left first, briskly moving across the lawn, and Duncan followed, stopping only long enough to pick up Edric's discarded suitcase. Edric moved next, turning at the hood of his car to scoop his jacket over his arm and to wait for Neal.

Was she telling the truth? he wondered. Had she forgotten everything that had happened between them?

"It seems to me that we had some pretty good memories," he recalled, deliberately lowering his deep voice to an intimate level.

19

Neal forced herself to shrug nonchalantly. "I suppose so."

She injected enough uninterest in her voice for Edric to peer suspiciously at her. There was no rancor in her answer, no bitterness that he could detect.

"But I'm sure," she continued "that most teen-agers have similar memories. Puppy love," she added. "We all experience it, live through it, and outgrow it."

"I wasn't a teen-ager," Edric snapped, upset over Neal's cool appraisal.

"I was," she returned. "Only seventeen. Too young to really know better. A child, you might say."

"You weren't a child," Edric returned sharply, not enjoying the swing of the conversation.

Neal chuckled softly, hoping that Edric would never see beyond this front of indifference.

"You seemed to enjoy it well enough," he countered.

"Then, yes," she agreed. "But now, probably not." Immediately she caught her mistake. There should have been no "probably" mentioned. She should have used an explicit "no."

Edric, however, didn't pick up on her slip at the moment. He was angry because she was treating the subject so lightly. Neal smiled when she saw the tightening of his facial muscles and the thinning of his mouth. Angry, she thought. Good! Perhaps she could add a little more wood to the fire of his frustration.

"How old were you, Edric?" She paused as if deep in thought. "Twenty-five or"—her voice drifted into silence as she pretended to ponder—"or were you twenty-six? You were so many years older than I."

"I was twenty-four then, and I'm thirty-seven now," he said gratingly, thoroughly displeased with Neal's sense of humor.

She softly laughed, following him in the house as Duncan held the door open.

"Like I said," Neal reiterated, moving into the air-conditioned coolness, "those memories belong to a *much* younger man and a starry-eyed teen-ager." Then a new spasm of giggles erupted, and Edric turned to scowl at her. "And if you weren't younger in years, you were perhaps . . . immature."

"And you sound like an old biddy," Edric barked irritably, moving past the grinning Duncan, yanking his suitcase from his hands.

Neal and Duncan both chuckled while Edric frowned. Clearly he was displeased with her frivolous reaction to his stroll down memory lane. But, she reasoned and rightly so, she had spent too many years getting over Edric Cameron to have these remembrances thrust into her face. Sure, she thought, walking into the large den, if she could just remember the happy ones, it would be okay, but with them came all the sad ones, sad ones that would cause old wounds to fester and run.

At the door that led into the hall outside the den, Edric stopped and looked at Neal. "Are you telling me that you don't remember at all?" The skepticism was indelibly stamped on his face.

Neal turned, glaring at him, wishing she could truthfully deny his accusation. She smiled instead, her eyes enigmatically changing from the bluish hue to a deep purple.

"I choose not to remember," she returned softly. "I've grown up, Edric. I'm not the seventeen-year-old child you remember."

They stood together at the entrance to the den by themselves. Molly and Duncan had disappeared into the kitchen, and Neal could hear the clink of the glasses and the ice. Edric's eyes stared through her indifference, and he reached her soul. When he spoke, his voice was tight and

21

heavy with sarcasm, but the volume never came above the throaty whisper.

"Don't keep throwing that child bit up to me. You may have been seventeen, but you weren't a child. You were a woman."

"Y'all come and get it," Molly called from the kitchen door, then moved briskly into the room. "I've got some of your favorite tea cakes, Neal."

Neal quickly averted her face, not willing for Edric to see her capitulation. Quickly she moved across the room and sat down on the sofa in front of the large oak table. She dropped her hat on the floor and held the cool glass in her hands. She fidgeted for a few minutes because she felt the heat of Edric's penetrating gaze.

"Well, Edric," Molly blurted with a laugh, "are ya gonna stand in the doorway and watch us, or are ya gonna come join us?"

Neal, unable to keep her eyes off him any longer, lifted her face and stared across the room. Edric's frame filled the doorway, his arms spread wide, his hands resting on each side of the jamb, the magnificent proportions of his physique clearly revealed to her. She had to admit that she had never met a man who stirred her as much as this man did.

"Neal," Duncan began, breaking the tense intimacy between them, "remember when you used to come here?" He shuffled around the room, finding himself an easy chair. "Many's the time that Molly fixed you them tea cakes and some lemonade."

Neal's eyes never left Edric's face, not even when he silently mouthed above Duncan's head, "Remember?"

"And remember that time—" Molly injected, lapsing into one of her stories.

All the time Edric leaned indolently against the door-jamb, the strong line of his jaw set, self-assured, arrogant.

22

His tawny eyes never left Neal, an enigmatic smile playing on his lips. He watched her smile, he watched her sip her lemonade, and he watched her eyes as they darted around the room, avoiding direct contact with him. He grinned. He knew she was remembering. There was no way she could get around it.

In one of the quiet moments, following Molly's story, Neal looked at Edric. She saw his mouth move: "Do you remember me at all?"

His words hadn't even been spoken, but they cut through the silence swiftly and surely, straight to Neal's heart. Edric chuckled softly, not waiting for an answer; rather, he walked down the hall to change his clothes. When he returned later, dressed in jeans and a cotton knit shirt, he accepted a tall glass of Molly's lemonade. With easy grace, he sat in one of the worn leather chairs that decorated the room.

Listening to the soft modulation of Molly's voice, Neal allowed herself to study the large room leisurely. This had been her favorite when she used to come to the Golden Cam, and she and Edric had spent many evenings here with his parents. Not a fancy house, she thought, but it had always been a home. She noticed the changes that Edric had made, and she had to compliment them. They added to the warmth of the house. Do you remember? Edric had asked. Dear God, she thought, how could she keep from remembering?

She laid her head against the back cushion and let her eyes fasten on the rock fireplace, remembering that particular winter evening so many years ago. Her first date with Edric. He'd taken her to his house after the football game, and it had begun storming as soon as they had arrived.

She could still see the flames as they danced up the chimney; she could still see the large rug that she and

Edric had been lying on. She could feel the warmth of the fire as it spread through her rain-soaked skin; she could feel the softness of the pillows; she could feel the tormenting nearness of Edric's body. She could hear the rain as it softly pattered aginst the windowpanes; she could hear Edric's deep voice as he whispered into her ear, "You've never been kissed before!" Such wonder; such awe.

She had shaken her head, glad that Edric would be the first, glad that she had waited. Her innocently sweet mouth parted as Edric's hand pushed the damp hair off her forehead, his fingers lingering on her flushed skin. Her blue-violet eyes, staring up into his face, were languid with desire.

One of his hands gently clasped her waist as the other roamed over her face, the soft pads of his fingers tracing the outline of her face, her eyebrows, her mouth. His golden eyes, also darkened with passion, hungrily feasted on the purity of her beauty. Slowly he leaned over her, one hand still spanning her waist, the other hand holding her chin.

"May I teach you?" he asked, knowing what her answer would be, knowing what her answer was. Lower the tenderly masculine face came, the lips hovering above hers.

"What about your mother and dad?" she had asked in a hoarse whisper, wanting to answer yes but afraid of her own unawakened responses, not understanding this desire that was ricocheting from one side of her veins to the other, from one end of her body to the other.

"We have plenty of time before they come in," he had answered, annoyed with her guileless question because it reminded him of his sullied intentions. "They stopped by the Hendrickses' for a while."

He had been trying to date her for weeks, ever since he'd first seen her. But she'd put him off. Finally he'd broken her resistance, and tonight he would taste her virginal

24

innocence; he would feast on the goodness of her lips, of her body, of her love. Greedily and selfishly he planned her seduction, movement by movement. Tonight was just the beginning.

His hands hadn't done a lot of exploring, she remembered. He'd known what he was doing. If he had awakened all her passionate desires at once, she would have retreated in fear. As it was, he carefully tutored her and slowly guided her into womanhood one step at a time. And this night he concentrated on teaching her all the intricacies of kissing.

New at the game of love, Neal hadn't known any better than to be truthful with Edric. "Please teach me," she begged, her hands shyly reaching up to touch the hard masculine face that peered into hers.

"I will, my little darling."

Their bodies touched only where his hand spanned her waist and where his lips touched hers. Breathy soft, his lips whispered across hers, dry, light caresses that innocently aroused. Again and again he had teased her like this until her hand clamped on the back of his head. She hadn't known exactly what she wanted, but she wanted more than this tormenting madness. He had played with her enough; she wanted him to capture and to hold her lips.

His hand left her waist and traveled to her mouth, still not touching any other part of her body intimately. He propped himself up on the other arm. His fingers played with her mouth, and finally his thumb slipped into one corner, parting her lips.

"I can hardly wait to taste your mouth," he said with a sigh, his voice thick, vibrating with his passion. "Really taste your mouth."

His lips lowered for the second time, finally conquering the territory. The tentative exploration was over and done with. His mouth parted, and he touched her lips, his lips moving on hers, gently, ever so gently, inviting hers to answer in kind. The warmth from his kiss began to fuse through her entire body, to ignite sensations she'd never known that she possessed. She tingled with an awareness of life that she'd never experienced before.

Her body began slowly to move under the tutelage of his lips, and she began to respond to him. Her hands voluntarily came up to tangle in the straight black hair, and her lips began to follow his lead, pressing against his, moving under his. She pleasured in the warm moistness; she pleasured in the stinging quivers that darted through her stomach to pierce that pristine membrane that separated her from womanhood, causing her to throb with instinctive desire.

When she was nauseated with wanting, when she moaned both her frustration and her pleasures, Edric's hand moved to her stomach, and his fingers splayed against its flat tautness. But he made no effort to insinuate his hand under the material of her blouse. He was content to move slowly. He would lingeringly savor all the experiences of making love to Neal. With deliberately planned movements, his hand gently kneaded the passion-tensed stomach muscles at the same time that his lips captured hers for that final assault.

"Oh, Edric," she whimpered hoarsely, "I didn't know it could be like this."

"It's beautiful to hold you like this, sweetheart," he said in return, "but it's going to be even better. I'm going to teach you how to enjoy and relish every second of making love, to delight in the taste and feel of love. You'll never have another lover like me."

At the moment Neal had been too dazed with passion to hear the cold edge of Edric's words. She had been too much in love to understand that he wanted only fulfillment. Naïvely she had assumed that he was in love with her as she was with him.

"I'll never need anyone but you," she had ignorantly murmured, her body half turning so that she was lying on her side, facing him, her hands running through his scalp, her fingers gently stimulating, caressively soft.

With his free hand he flattened her body to the floor, and he leaned over her again, his hard body partially covering hers. Inundated with a flood of new sensations and not understanding them, Neal pressed against his chest with both hands. He had moved too quickly, and he had frightened her.

"Don't, Edric," she had cried, tears shimmering in her eyes. "I—please don't kiss me anymore."

"Would you like another glass of lemonade?"

The question startled Neal from her ruminations, and she jerked her head in the direction of the voice. Her blue-violet eyes, dusky with remembrances, guiltily caught the amber ones, and she blushed a deep pink. Hastily she looked at the empty glass that she held in her hand.

"Would you like some more lemonade, Neal?" Edric repeated in an amused voice.

Neal smiled, composed herself, and shook her head. "No, thanks. This break's been pleasant, but I'm afraid I've work to do. Another time."

Edric wondered if there would be another time. He was afraid not, so he pressed. "Just one more in memory of us"—his voice lowered—"you and me."

Neal steeled her emotions and forced herself to chuckle quietly. "Okay, Edric," she acquiesced, "one more for memory's sake." Her words tumbled out, and she had to laugh at the expectancy on Edric's face. "In memory of" —she paused dramatically—"of Molly's excellent lemonade, which I haven't forgotten."

27

A little less than pleased with her humor at his expense but glad that she was staying longer, Edric took the glass that she held out to him and walked across the hardwood floor. As he moved, Neal watched, drinking in everything about him: his legs, lean and muscular, the tapered waist and hips, the muscular arms and shoulders. He was altogether a vital, powerful-looking man.

As if he were aware of her scrutiny, his head swerved suddenly, and he stared at her. His lips parted, and his rough-soft tongue—she could feel the rough tenderness of it now—came out to glaze his firm mouth with a fiery nectar. Not conscious of her reaction, Neal opened her mouth, letting her tongue touch her lips.

When he smiled, Neal quickly turned her head, hiding her errant feelings and her temporary lapse into the past. She had remembered more than she wanted to; she had been with him longer than she should have. It would have been much wiser if she hadn't come. With a start she realized that he and she were alone and almost jumped when Edric spoke to her again.

"What brought you back to the hill country?" he asked, having filled both glasses.

Neal shrugged, taking hers, watching him as he settled back, ensconcing himself in the large chair. "I wanted to come home," she answered truthfully, having learned a long time ago it was easier to be truthful in the long run. "I learned while I was doing my residency in Beaumont that I'm not cut out for pampered poodles and Siamese. And when I met Sam at a conference in Houston, and he offered me this job . . ." She shrugged, letting her voice trail into silence, lifting her drink to her mouth, enjoying the tangy lemonade.

"You don't find Kerrville too small and drab for your city tastes now?" he questioned.

"I don't suppose I'll ever get the hill country out of my

28

blood," Neal replied slowly, "and no, I don't find Kerr-ville too drab for my tastes. I'm rather fond of small towns."

"I'm glad you came home," Edric said, his eyes suggestively darting to the fireplace.

Not pretending to misunderstand him, Neal laughed. "I'm glad I came home, too, Edric. But I didn't come home because I wanted to relive my past." The musical tones of her laughter followed her words. "It happened too long ago to matter now."

"How many years?" he asked, knowing full well that it had been about thirteen.

"Let's see," she parried, playing his game. "It doesn't seem like it's been that long, does it?"

"No," he replied slowly, "it doesn't." His eyes searched Neal's face, and he asked, "Do you think it's too late to renew an old acquaintance?"

Neal shook her head. "No, it's not too late to renew old friendship." She saw the hope that flared in his eyes. "But it's too late to revive the flames of an old romance when there's nothing left."

"I'm not quite sure that's the case," Edric softly returned, positive that Neal had remembered that first night when they had lain in front of the fireplace. The first time he had kissed her, the first time any man had.

"I'm sure," she said firmly. Her blue-violet eyes reflected nothing contrary to what she was saying. "I wouldn't have come back if it weren't over and done with."

Edric lifted the glass to his lips, wishing it were something stronger than lemonade. Neal's proclamation was cold, final!

"Has there been someone else in your life?" he asked curiously.

She nodded, leaning her head on the cushioned back of the sofa. "There has."

29

She deliberately didn't tell him more. The memory of Tom could still hurt her. She'd never forget the days and nights she'd spent with him after the plane crash, and she'd never forget the last time she'd seen him before the accident. He had ridden away on his motorcycle, turning to wave a kiss in her direction. She didn't see him again until he was lying in the intensive care unit of the hospital.

"Serious?" Edric asked, jealousy tearing at his soul, cutting him to shreds.

"Yes," she returned in a low, evenly modulated voice, the anguish causing the edges to be ragged and raw. "Both of us were studying to be vets." She stopped talking and chewed on her bottom lip. "We were to have been married after we graduated, but"—her throat constricted with her tears—"he was killed in a plane crash. He was taking flying lessons—" She couldn't continue.

"I'm sorry," Edric murmured, knowing his words were empty, but they were all he had. And she wouldn't have accepted more.

Neal took several gulps of her drink. "I think," she began, wiping a stray tear from her cheek, "the worst part was the waiting and the watching after the accident."

"He didn't die immediately?" Edric questioned not callously but deliberately.

He sensed her distress, and he knew from his own past experience that once you'd bared your soul and shed your burden, the pain was eased. Then the healing could begin. He remembered how he'd felt when first his mother and then his father had died. He remembered the grief that had finally erupted the night he had cried like a baby in Duncan's arms.

Neal shook her head. "No." Her lips quivered, and her chin trembled. "He was badly hurt and all mangled up. There was no hope." She sniffed and wiped her hand

30

across her eyes. "He awakened one time and recognized me." She paused and drew a ragged, painful breath. "He told me that he loved me, and while he was holding my hand, he went into a coma. He never awakened again."

Both of them sat in the quietness of the room for a long time, neither speaking. Finally Edric moved from his chair and walked into the kitchen. While he was gone, Neal carried her glass to the bar. She was standing by the patio door, staring blindly onto the lawn when Edric returned.

"Molly wants to know if you'll stay for supper?"

Neal was about to shake her head, but Edric spoke again.

"Please, Neal. I'm sorry I upset you." His apology was simple but tender. "I don't want you to drive yourself home like this. Not until you feel better."

He stood behind her, and his hands gently clasped her shoulders. "I know sorta how you feel," he went on. "When Mom and Dad—"

"I know," Neal whispered, "Sam told me about it." She turned to look him in the face. "It hurt me, Edric," she confessed in a low voice. "I loved them so much." Tears shone in her eyes.

He caught her in his arms and held her tightly, each of them consoling the other, each of them seeking strength from the other. Although they had been separated by the miles and the years, both had suddenly come home. Both had found a haven of refuge for their anguished souls.

"Neal, I'd like us to—"

She shook her head against his chest before he could complete his statement.

"It wouldn't work, Edric," she replied in a muffled tone. "I don't want to try to dig up the past. It's never the same."

"I don't want the past, Neal. I want us to take today and

the next day, one at a time." His voice was a husky whisper, low and vibrant, warming her, urging her to feel again, to imagine, and hope. "Can't we try, Neal?"

She shook her head adamantly. She didn't want want any more sorrow in her life. She'd gone through a heartbreak with Edric and that had left her a half woman, and she'd just put herself together when Tom died. After that she had retreated from any emotional involvement. She wouldn't allow herself to be hurt again. She wouldn't consider running the risk of being hurt again. And Edric certainly was the only man who could hurt her. She knew that now.

"Is there someone else in your life now?"

"Sorta."

"Who?" He waited tensely for the answer.

"Kerry Baxter."

"Another veterinarian?"

She shook her head, pushed out of his arms, moved around the room, her arms crossed over her chest. "He's an accountant."

"You love him?"

Neal didn't answer his question. "I'm seriously thinking about marrying him."

"Does he live in Beaumont?" Edric walked to the bar and began to stack the empty glasses on the tray.

When she waited so long to answer, he turned his head and caught her eyes. She nodded.

"Why did you leave then and come back home if you were thinking about marrying him?" Edric asked, his eyes slitted, a speculative gleam in them. He picked up the tray and turned to face her.

"I wanted to come home to think about it," she replied truthfully. "I wanted to give myself a chance."

"Evidently you don't love him," Edric said in surmise,

a faint hopefulness curving his lips into a smile.

Surprisingly she agreed with him. "No, I don't love him. That's why I want to think it over."

Now it was Edric's turn to be surprised or, perhaps, startled. He set the tray down with a thud; the glasses rolled on their bases precariously before they finally stood still. He glowered at her, his hands dropping to his hips.

"Why are you planning to marry him if you don't love him?"

Neal smiled tightly. "I'm thirty, Edric, in case you've forgotten, and I'm ready to settle down with a husband and a family." She raised her brows dramatically. "I do want children."

"My God!" He wheezed vehemently. "It sounds like you're marrying him for stud service."

"Really! Now that sounds more like the Edric Cameron I remember." Then she quietly said, "Don't point a finger at me, Edric. At least I'm being truthful to him and to myself."

Edric's brow clouded with the fury of his anger, and his voice thundered when he spoke. "I'm not pointing a finger at you," he said. "I just don't see how you can be so cold and logical about a move like marriage."

"*You* don't have to see," Neal retaliated. "This is entirely between Kerry and me. You're not involved in it at all."

Her words stung. How coolly she dismissed him. He wanted to take hold of her shoulders and shake her. I am involved, he wanted to say. From the minute I set eyes on you, Neal, I've been part of you and you've been part of me. But he only glared back at her, his arms crossed over his broad chest, his mouth set in a tight line.

Neal shook her head, the loose curls bobbing around her face. "I'm only here because of my job," she continued. "And may I kindly point out," she went on in

33

smooth, even sarcasm, "that my deliberation about marriage is far more respectable than your cold-blooded seduction of me was."

Edric winced inwardly at her words, coming to stand closer to her. "If you're marrying just to have a home and a bunch of kids," he asserted with equal sarcasm, "why not marry just any man who happens to come along?"

Neal began to chuckle softly, but the sound continued to grow louder with her humor. "Are you proposing after all these years, Edric?"

He blinked his eyes several times and stared at her blankly. He hadn't been, because his marriage had been less than pleasant. But even as a joke the thought of his marrying her seemed a better idea than her marriage to this Baxter fellow. He glared at her, shocked at the turn his own thoughts had taken, wondering why he'd allowed himself to get all worked up like this. He was angry with himself for having let old feelings resurrect themselves with such forcefulness.

He shrugged and grinned. "Sorry, I shouldn't have butted into your personal affairs."

He walked to the fireplace and placed one hand on the mantel. Why did he want to rekindle an old affair? he wondered. Sure, he'd been bored with life for a long time, but it didn't call for this. His eyes raked over Neal's face, the short black curls that massed around her face, back to the eyes.

"Why'd you cut your hair?" he asked abruptly.

The question threw her off guard, the change was so quick. "My work," she said absently. "It's easier for me to keep it like this than to have it falling in my face all the time."

He nodded.

"What about you, Edric?" Neal asked.

34

Edric's brows furrowed in question.

"What's happened to you during the past years?"

He grinned. "Time for my confession?"

She nodded her head, flashing her even white teeth in her smile. "It's good for the soul."

"Not much," he murmured gruffly. "One brief marriage that was hell. Turned the ranch into an animal preserve." He smiled. "Guess that's about all."

"Divorced?" Neal asked, her heart hurting as it hadn't hurt since she'd learned that Edric didn't love her.

He nodded. "We decided to go our separate ways."

"How long ago?"

"About three years."

"No children?"

"No children." He waited for the next question. "No more?"

"No more." She grinned. "If I'm going to stay for dinner, I'd like to bathe some of this grime away. Do you think Molly will lend me a clean outfit to wear for the evening?"

Edric's eyes lit up with the news. "We'll find out real quick. But if she doesn't," he added, "you can wear one of my shirts." The flickering light in his eyes dared her to remember.

She swallowed and nodded. "Fine." But she didn't move.

"Need any help finding the bathroom?" he asked.

Neal shook her head. "No, I think I can find it. If I can't, I'll call Molly." She chuckled. "I would like to have the clean clothes before I go into the bathroom, please."

"I planned to bring them to you later," he said, teasing her softly.

"Not this time," came the firm rejoinder.

"Next time perhaps." His faint words and his soft

35

laughter engulfed her as Edric walked out of the den into the kitchen. When he returned, he had Molly in tow.

"So you need some clean clothes," Molly briskly announced. "Well, just follow me, and we'll see what we can find."

"Remember, Neal," Edric called after her, "if you need help, just call for me."

CHAPTER TWO

Neal stepped out of the shower, drying her body with a large green towel, enjoying the fluffy softness against her damp skin. When she had it securely tucked around her midsection, sarong style, she took the extra towel and twisted it like a turban around her mass of wet curls. She'd rub them dry in a few minutes.

"Take your time," Molly had instructed, laying the white dress on the bed along with a delicate lace slip. "Supper won't be for another couple of hours." She went on to explain the delay. "That group from San Antonio was delayed, and they just called from town saying they were on their way, so Edric and Duncan will show them around the campgrounds before we eat."

Neal nodded her acknowledgment. "As soon as I dress, I'll come help you with dinner."

"Absolutely not," Molly had enjoined briefly. "I still don't like meddlers in my kitchen when I work." The semblance of a smile that twisted her lips took the sharpness out of her words. "We'll have the house to ourselves for a while, so you can rest if you like." With these few comments Molly had marched out of the room, leaving Neal to herself.

Neal slipped on underwear, dropping the slip over her head. Then she pulled on the loose Mexican-made dress, walking to the mirror that stood grandly in the corner of the room. She lifted her hands and adjusted the neckline so that it hung correctly, and she stood for a long time, studying herself in the mirror.

Because she and Molly were about the same weight and height, the dress fitted well, but Neal wondered if it had been a good idea for her to borrow it. She could tell that Edric was in one of his reckless moods. He was determined to resurrect the desire that had flowed so violently and undammed between them years ago. Even if he couldn't revive it, he intended to give it his best try. It was his ego, urging him on. That was all. The same reason he had pursued her so many years ago. Pure, unadulterated male ego. And this dress didn't help the situation one bit.

The white material was soft and gauzy, falling gently from her shoulders, loosely engulfing her body. The scooped neckline was adorned with hand-embroidered flowers in white silk, which added a richness to the otherwise plain dress. The small cap sleeves accented Neal's length of tanned arm. The effect was pristine yet alluring. Sensual yet innocent. It would remind Edric of . . . Well, never mind what it would remind him of, Neal thought. Wearing this pure white dress was like waving a red flag in front of a bull.

A little later, as she combed her hair, she heard the light taps on the door. Without moving her body, just turning her head in the direction, she answered.

"Yes?"

"Are you dressed?" Edric's voice filtered through the thick door.

"Yes," Neal replied, turning around, facing the door.

"May I come in?"

Again the one word: "Yes."

The door swung open, and Edric's large frame was inside the room, exuding his full masculinity. As if she hadn't seen him for a long time, Neal's eyes hungrily

38

moved over him, visually tasting his virility, glutting on the handsomeness of his broad shoulders that she'd vainly sought for in other men. She remembered the wiry crispness of the hair that shaded the muscles of his broad chest. She remembered the feel of his hardness; she felt the soft pads of her fingers, running over his chest, his stomach, his abdomen. . . .

When her eyes hit that familiar brass buckle on his belt, Neal lifted her face and stared boldly into his face. In his eyes she saw his anguish; his undisguised hunger frightened her. The wanting haunted his eyes, exposing his fevered desire. But that was all Neal saw—desire, no love.

"I like the dress," he said softly, his hands casually hanging by his sides as he moved into the room, closer to her.

She smiled her thanks, moving away from his nearness, walking to the side of the bed to slip her feet into the leather thongs that Molly had also lent her.

His breathing heightened as he studied the color of the dress, the soft gauzy fabric, and the newness. As quickly his mind began to wander randomly in the verdant meadows of his memories.

"You're beautiful," he confessed in the same quiet voice. "Really beautiful."

"Thanks," she murmured, not daring to look into his face, not willing to share her feelings with him at the moment.

She'd walked this path with him once before, and she knew all the promises, the flattery, the looks, the touches. She understood the heartache and the pain when it was over. She had lived with the wound for thirteen years, and she didn't plan to incur any more battle scars.

That's why she could accept what Kerry was offering, peace and tranquillity, a home and a family. Each was willing to make a commitment to the other. She had to agree that there was no great passion flaring between them, but they could cultivate that, she thought. Or learn to live without it. After all, desire was only a small part of marriage.

"I'm going to show the old house and campgrounds to a group from San Antonio. Want to go with me?"

Neal's inclination was to jerk her head up and to stare into Edric's face. Dear God, she wanted to shout, what do you take me for? She didn't want to go to the old house. She didn't want to go anywhere near the river. Memories were already washing in on her. What would happen if she went to the river? What would happen if she went to the willow trees? Surely he knew what he was asking her to do. It was almost enough to make her hate him.

His voice was low, and Neal could hear the dull throb of pain as he spoke. "I'd like you to come with me, Neal. You can look around by yourself while I show the men around."

He waited for her answer. God, but he wanted her to come. Odd, he thought, until a couple of hours ago she'd been a dim part of his memory, and now quite suddenly she was so much the essence of his thoughts. He wanted to be with her, and his mind and body, as if addicted, craved her presence. It was as if he'd found a part of himself that had been missing.

If she didn't go, she reasoned, bending over, her fingers touching the leather straps that crossed her feet, he would know that she feared meeting the past, that she still remembered the sweetness and the intimacy of the place. If she didn't go, Edric would have another weapon to use against her.

Whereas, if she went, only she would know that she'd never forgotten the man, the place, or the time. The memory was like a beautiful painting that she'd framed and hung in the gallery of time. It was a sacred possession, a highly treasured possession. At first she had come back frequently to look at it, but as the years passed, she came less frequently. Yet it was cherished and loved.

Standing up, she pushed all this suffocating nostalgia from her mind, smiled, and forced a certain amount of coolness to her words.

"I'd love to come, Edric. The old ranch house was always a favorite haunt of mine." She walked across the room toward him. "Has it changed much during the years?"

He nodded, the tawny eyes scrutinizing the woman who looked so ethereal and illusive. Could she be an hallucination? he wondered. Would she disappear into nowhere as suddenly as she had appeared?

"It's changed." He saw the disappointment that filled those expressive eyes. "Part of it has been turned into a kitchen and dining hall for the campers."

Sadly she said, "Time changes all things, doesn't it?" As if she had been trying to reach back in time herself, she added, "It's never the same, is it?"

"No." The quiet answer was soft and soothing to her sorrow. "But we wouldn't want it to be the same. Yesterday's experience isn't large enough or good enough for us today because we're different."

She disagreed with him. She would have accepted his love. It was good enough for her; their love would have grown and matured with the passing of time.

"It was good for yesterday," he said. "Today we need something else."

She shrugged indifferently. "You're probably right."

The subject dropped as she followed him out of the room down the hall into the den. Although she was enjoying her evening with the Marshes and although she was glad that she'd seen Edric again, she would be glad when the night was done. She didn't know how much longer she

41

could wade through all this emotional sentimentality without breaking.

Edric stopped by the cedar rack near the door and donned his hat, turning to speak to Duncan, who was waiting for him. "Neal and I will meet you at the old place. As soon as Warner and his group get here, you can drive them up."

Duncan nodded his head, his experienced eyes taking in the young couple who stood in front of him. His rough and work-calloused hand adjusted the brim of the old hat.

"I want to show Neal all the changes that we've made, and I want her to see my stock." As old as he was, Edric almost squirmed under the all-knowing look that Duncan cast at him.

Duncan grinned, knowing that Edric was proud of his animal refuge, but he also knew that Edric wanted Neal's company more than he wanted to show off the sanctuary.

"Sure, boss. See ya later."

Not long afterward, sitting in Edric's truck, jostling along the rough roads that circled the large foothills, Neal savored the beauty of the hill country. She loved the sprawling cedar trees that spanned the countryside, and she loved the river that lazily zigzagged through the ranch. She watched the evening sun as it cast its gentle hues on the beauties of earth.

"I love this country," she said reverently. "It has a beauty that no other place has."

"I agree," Edric concurred, never taking his eyes off the winding road that first scaled the foothill, then descended sharply. At the bottom of the last curve they passed several of the ranch houses.

"Do Molly and Duncan still live here?" Neal asked as they passed a small stone bungalow, nestled in the midst of the cedar trees.

"No," Edric answered. "They live in the main house now. I asked them to move up there when Alexa left."

"Alexa Stimpson?" Neal asked.

She could easily recall the beautiful redhead. Tall, willowy, worldly-wise. She could remember the first time she saw Alexa. The older woman had never uttered one word to Neal, yet the seventeen-year-old had known that Alexa wanted Edric. And, Neal thought, she got him. Naturally she wondered what had happened to break up their marriage.

"Our relationship," Edric began as if in answer to Neal's thoughts, "drifted into marriage. After Dad . . ."

He didn't complete his statement, and Neal could understand why.

"Alexa and I became closer. I thought it was more than sexual attraction." He seemed to be speaking to himself more than to Neal. "She was there when I needed her."

So was I, Neal cried silently, but you didn't want me.

Unaware of Neal's deep-seated jealousy, Edric continued, "She was so sweet and warm at first."

I'll bet, Neal thought, seething.

"Right after Mom's death she seemed to be so understanding and comforting."

Spare me, Neal snapped to herself. I knew the woman better than you did.

"I really thought we could be happy together, Neal. And at that time I thought I loved her, and I did want to marry her."

Neal nodded, turning her head to look out the window, biting back the tears. She could understand his feelings. That's the way she had felt about Tom. She had thought she loved him, and though her feelings for him were different from those which she had felt for Edric, she had believed that they could have a wonderful and full life together.

"But," Edric continued, his voice hardening, "it wasn't long after the honeymoon that Alexa began to show her true colors."

She lasted longer than I would have figured, Neal thought.

"Life out here didn't suit her, and she had a hankering for the glamour of city lights." He shrugged. "I guess I was too caught up in my grief to think it through because I knew what kind of person she was when I married her."

Neal waited quietly to see if he'd talk more, but when he didn't, she asked, "What happened then, Edric?"

"From there we drifted into the phase called you-do-your-own-thing-and-I'll-do-mine." Bitterness coated the words.

"How long were you married?" Her eyes never left the rugged terrain.

"Three years," he replied, clearly closing the conversation, giving his full attention to his driving.

The truck bounced to the bottom of the hill over the bumpy road, and Edric turned to maneuver into the shallow-watered riverbed. Nearly a quarter of a mile later he drove out of the river, and they wound around another hill until they reached the old ranch house, which lay sheltered in a grove of cedar trees.

"Here it is," he announced, braking the truck, pulling the key from the ignition.

"It hasn't changed much from the outside," Neal commented, that faraway look in her eyes.

She opened her door, climbed out of the truck, and walked across the grass toward the house. Although a huge outdoor dining hall with a brick floor and a cedar arbor had been built next to the main house, none of the trees had been cut down. Rather, the structure had been built around them.

Edric lazily followed her, watching her reactions more than he looked at the camp. He, too, loved the ranch, all three thousand acres, but he couldn't afford to let sentimentality blind him. The day of the big spreads was coming to an end, and he had to update his holdings so that he could continue to earn a living. A large portion, therefore, he had converted into campgrounds, which he rented or leased to different groups during the year. Of course, the majority of these people came in the spring and summer, but there were always the few who came during the winter, closing up in the intimacy of the main lodge.

First Neal walked up the wooden steps onto the small porch; then she pushed on the screen door and stepped into the serving bar of the kitchen, which had been enlarged for group dining. She crossed over the hardwood floors until she stood in the living room, looking at the new sofas and chairs that curved around the huge rock fireplace.

"The original kitchen, dining room, and the two front bedrooms were converted into the kitchen and serving area," she observed, her eyes scanning the complex.

Edric nodded. "We've built a lot of dormitories around the recreation area, and this is used only for the dining hall. We kept the large hall, so the groups can get together during the evenings for whatever."

"Do you regret having to do it?" Neal asked, a tear in her voice.

Edric walked to one of the windows and stared out, looking at the white cliff that rose from behind the river, spearing into the blueness of the sky. Did he regret having to do it? Yes, he regretted it. He had always enjoyed the solitude of the old house and the tranquillity of the clear, cool water of the river.

45

The decision had been tough, but it was one that had to be made. His father, Pierce Cameron, had wrested with it for several years, and at his death he had handed the problem to Edric. Later Alexa had nagged him to sell the land, but he couldn't part with it. It was an integral part of him, and he wanted it. But it was serving few in its present state.

Then he had begun a sanctuary for the protection of endangered species of animals, pouring all his energy and money into the campaign. He had refused to renew hunting leases and instead had begun renting the property to groups that wanted to retreat from city life. During the past few years he and Duncan had modernized the facilities, and they were actually breaking even financially.

"Yes, I regretted it," he finally admitted, "but at least my animals are safe, and many people are able to enjoy this great beauty. Perhaps in time to come it will pay for itself."

"I think perhaps I would have been selfish," Neal murmured. "I don't know that I would have trusted people with my land."

"Most of the time we do what we have to do," he explained quietly. "This was one of the things I felt compelled to do. And it was one of the things that Alexa didn't want me to do." He smiled sadly. "It was perhaps the one quarrel we never resolved. She couldn't understand my preoccupation with this spread and the stock."

Neal laughed. "I'm glad you hung on. At least Sam and I will never be without a job as long as the Golden Cam is around." She walked to the row of windows that crossed the front of the building and looked at the rugged terrain. "Is that a herd of horses back there?" she asked, straining her eyes to see.

Edric smiled, moving behind her, peering over her shoulder. "Wild ones," he told her. "They've been grazing

46

the land for about ten years now." He tapped her shoulder and pointed into the shelter of trees. "And look over there."

Neal turned her head and looked at the deer that gracefully trekked over the grass-covered land. "Oh, Edric, this is so beautiful." She spun around to find herself in his arms.

It wasn't an intentional move on his part; it wasn't a planned reaction for her. It was accidental, but neither made an effort to rectify the mistake. They stood staring at each other. Both wondered if it would be possible to stop the clock, to turn the hands back, to pick up the threads of their feelings for each other where they had been severed.

His hands closed around her body, and he pulled her closer. She didn't resist; willingly she swayed nearer, letting the fullness of her breasts press against his chest. The color of her eyes deepened until they were purple, and they gazed into the face that hovered above hers. Her hands traveled the familiar route, closing around his neck, her fingers playing in the thick black hair.

Higher her fingers moved in frenzied pitch to spread through his hair, the tips kneading the scalp, mussing the thickness as they inched to his face and cupped the bronzed perfection. Her mouth, hungry for the taste of him, feathered over his lips, his chin, sampling first, then thoroughly reacquainting herself with his lips.

"So beautiful," he murmured as she nipped on the fullness of his bottom lip. "So very beautiful."

Her hands tightened on the base of his neck, and she urged his mouth to hers, her lips parting for the touch. His mouth, passionate and tender, caught hers hungrily, and his hands moved over her back, arching her, pressing her breasts into even closer contact with his body. His

47

tongue's sweet probing poignantly reminded her of that deeper invasion.

These first intimate moments with him were treasured memories that Neal would place in her gallery, displaying them with the others. Knowing this, she could accept what Edric was offering; she could give Edric what he wanted. Knowing this and accepting it, she could take what she wanted and needed.

His hand moved around her back, under her arm, cupping one of her breasts, and with great urgency his mouth bore down on hers. His tongue moved inside her mouth, exploring all the sweetness, all the nooks and niches of delight. As if they had never been separated, she squirmed closer to him, eagerly learning his body again, her hand stroking the muscular cords of his shoulders.

"Neal," he whispered, lifting his lips slightly, "I'm so glad you came back home, and I'm so glad you came back to me." His warm breath was honey spilling against her creamy flesh, slowly oozing like fan tracery; wider and wider the circle grew.

Did I come back for you? she whispered to herself, the thought tumbling hazily about in that region called her mind, but she couldn't quite get it all together. And it could, therefore, never make it to her lips. But she didn't worry about it; she wasn't concerned with logic at the moment. Her heart pounded, and her entire body was aflame with only those feelings that Edric could generate. She arched her neck, and Edric's lips began to caress the silken curve.

Against the smooth satin of her shoulder, Edric's lips moved, savoring her sweet warmth, sending renewed shivers of ecstasy through her body. "Stay with me tonight, Neal." The plea was a hushed whisper. Had he said it? Had she imagined that he said it?

The answer was lost in the blaring honk of Duncan's

jeep as it rounded the sharp curve. Neal quickly disentangled herself from Edric's hold and moved across the room, running her fingers through her hair. Womanlike, her fingers darted to the neck of her dress, pulling and tugging, checking to see that it was hanging right. Then she looked across the room at the man who was still standing next to the window, the evening sunlight spilling around him.

Even though his face was shadowed because the sun was to his back, Neal could see the questions that furrowed his brow. He wondered if she regretted having kissed him or not. He wondered if she was angry or embarrassed. He had known the young Neal well and could read her, but this Neal was different. He wasn't sure about her at all. He'd have to learn her all over again.

Neal's lips, tingling from the kiss, quirked into a lovely smile. "I'm not sorry it happened," she admitted, watching Duncan and the men as they approached the house. "I wanted it as much as you did."

Edric misunderstood her confession and heard more than he should have. She could see the triumph as it brightly flicked into life in the depth of the golden brown orbs, lighting his face with that arrogance Neal had known too well already. As usual, she thought, he's concerned only with his wants and needs.

Not letting her smile die, Neal quietly walked to where Edric stood and put her hands on his face, again cupping the bronzed cheeks. "I wanted to see if we still . . . reacted the same way to one another. Just checking out the body chemistry," she said with a chuckle. "We still create quite an explosion!"

Edric tensed but didn't smile. "Just an experiment!" Anger surged through the hard frame.

Neal grinned, pleased with herself. "Not really. It just happened, and I'm glad it did."

49

The men were close enough to the building that Neal and Edric could hear the low drone of their voices. Edric knew they would soon lose the intimacy of the moment, so he said, "Now that you're aware of your physical attraction to me, I see nothing that stands in the way of our getting together."

Neal's laughter was spontaneous and bubbling. "No, Edric, you and I are not going to get together, as you put it. My life is sorted out, and that's the way it's going to remain." She dropped her hands from his face and stepped backward. "I won't go to bed with any man until I decide what I intend to do about Kerry."

"Not even with poor Kerry?" Edric asked with impetuous audacity.

The door opened, and Duncan walked in, followed by two strangers. Neal, looking over her shoulder, quickly stepped out of the way, answering in an undertone. "That, Edric Cameron, is my business."

Edric looked at her and grinned, exhilaration speeding through his body, pumping excitement into every inch of him. She had always had this effect on him. He chuckled softly and walked toward the men who followed Duncan into the room. Holding his hand out in greeting, he spoke.

"Hello, I'm Edric Cameron, owner of the Golden Cam."

As the men engaged first in desultory comments, Neal walked through the house out the back entrance and moved to the banks of the clear light-green river. She stood for endless seconds, thinking about the times that she and Edric had swum here. Her head turned, and she looked down the river, squinting. Were they still there?

Soundlessly she began to step over the rocky surface, headed for the trees that drooped their branches over the river. Again she was guided by an instinct stronger than reason. She never thought about Edric and the men in the house; she didn't think about the consequences of her visit.

She rounded the bend, and she saw them: the tall willow trees with their heavily laden branches swaying and dipping into the water, their foliage just a shade greener than the river. She should have stopped; she should have returned, but she did neither. Her feet never missed a step, and she continued to move nearer the grove of trees.

Soon she was sheltered under the branches, sunshine mottling her face as it pierced through the thick leafage in places. She moved closer to one of the larger trunks, and she leaned against it, her eyes darting around as if she were looking for something in particular.

And perhaps she was. Maybe in the back of her mind she was searching for that Neal she'd left behind when she had finished school and moved away. Maybe she was searching for that love she thought she had for Edric. Her thoughts clouded with questions. She asked herself the same question that Edric had. Why had she come home?

Edric had been right about one thing. If she had intended to marry Kerry, she wouldn't have given up her job in Beaumont and come running home. No, she admitted finally, she hadn't come home to think about it. She'd come home for another reason. And she had even hidden this from herself until she met Edric, more specifically until she had allowed him to kiss her.

She paced back and forth, looking from one tree to another, running her fingers up and down the rough bark, wondering if their tree was still standing. As frequently as the hill country was flooded, she wouldn't have been surprised to find it gone. If it was standing, she wondered, were their initials still there?

Then she saw it; then she felt the deeply etched letters, hewn as if to withstand time. And she remembered that day when Edric had carved them there, that afternoon when he had first told her that he loved her. She recalled the special beauty of that early spring day.

Everything had seemed perfect to her. The sun had almost disappeared from sight, and its golden colors splayed across the sky, its magnificence winging down on the two of them. A gentle breeze had wafted through the trees, and the leaves had sung a song while the branches had gently swayed to and fro. Even the water had danced, tiny ripples pirouetting over the surface.

Edric had brought her to the old house for a picnic, so he said, and at the time she had believed him. Later she had realized that the picnic was just a guise for other plans. His primary purpose had been to make love to her. And he had.

It hadn't taken him as long to change as it had her, and he waited on the banks of the river, allowing her all the time she needed. Young and naïve, she had thought it was consideration and love on his part. Later she realized that it was just part of the great master plan for seduction.

She had stepped out the back door barefoot, clad only in the purple bikini. Her long black hair, French-braided, fell down her back in one thick plait. Her tall, supple body, lightly and evenly tanned, gleamed copper in the late-afternoon sun. Even at seventeen she had known that she would go to bed with Edric, that she would make love to him. At seventeen she knew that she loved Edric. And as she walked across the yard, she knew this was the moment.

Rather than its frightening her as it had done in the beginning, however, it now filled her with exhilaration and exultation. Her love for Edric had moved her out of childhood; she was now a woman in all respects but one. And there was no other man in the world whom she would have chosen to escort her to womanhood but Edric.

When she first walked up to him, his back was to her,

both hands resting casually on his hips, and all she could see was the long-tailed yellow shirt that dangled loosely from his shoulders, unbuttoned, moving gently in the breeze. Her eyes feasted on the curves of his thigh muscles and on the broad shoulders that stretched the soft material of the shirt covering his torso.

Then he heard her, and he turned around, his golden brown eyes hungrily gorging on her beauty. Her bathing suit accented the full swell of her creamy breasts and the gentle curves of her hips. Her skin was smooth and coppery. The muscles in her thighs flexed as she drew nearer to him, and her mouth parted, her lips pouting provocatively, asking for his kisses.

Her eyes, a deep blue-violet, moved from the shock of black hair to the chest, shadowed with dark hair, to the flat-muscled stomach, lower to the navel. Then the plane of bronzed skin ended, disappearing into a pair of brown swim trunks that snugged the contours of his hips. Down her eyes swept again, devouring the hair-covered, sinewy legs that had begun moving in her direction.

His arms went around her, and his resolve to spend the earlier part of the day picnicking and swimming fled. Edric hungered only for Neal; he wanted her as he had wanted no other woman. His insatiable hunger was partly because Neal was a virgin, and he had waited so long, holding back until it seemed he couldn't last another day. But partly it was because he was seeing no other woman but her. He just hadn't wanted to. The combination had pushed him to the limit, and he wanted Neal. He wanted her right now.

His hand slipped over the satin smoothness of her skin, his fingers spreading into the small of her back, the tips sliding under the band of the bikini. Each fingertip felt like a hot coal of fire on Neal's skin, and no pressure was needed to urge her closer to Edric's heated frame.

Her hands wrapped around his back, and her fingers began to tease the muscle-corded shoulders, tracing intricate designs on the soft material of his shirt. But she wasn't content with touching him through the material. She wanted to feel his skin bare to her touch.

With great daring Neal had pulled out of his arms and had pushed her hands under the shirt, shoving it off his shoulders, letting it drop at his feet. Then she placed her hands on his shoulders, the palms gently moving in a circular pattern, the fingers teasingly soft. She smiled when she saw the flames leaping higher and higher in Edric's eyes.

His head had lowered, and his mouth had taken possession of hers, his warm and wet lips covering hers, drinking of that sweet wine of purity that flowed from the pure well of her soul. His tongue, sure of the territory, darted, skimmed, teased, and filled, awakening the passion that he knew flowed so freely for him.

His hand dropped from the small of her back to her buttocks, cupping the generous fullness. His lean and tactile fingers pressed through the soft fabric of the bikini as he cradled her firmly tender curves to his throbbing frame. In answer to the overt sensuality of his movement, Neal's hands glided to his waist, her fingers slipping beneath the band of his trunks.

She felt Edric's stomach muscles as they tensed, and she felt the quick inhalation of his breath. New at the art of seduction, she wasn't sure whether to proceed, so she stopped moving her hands, but instinctively she began to rotate her lower body, pressing against him, gently arousing him.

He lifted his lips and huskily whispered in her ears, "Don't stop touching me, sweetheart. Please don't stop. I like the feel of your hands on me, and I like you to touch me."

Intoxicated with love and drugged with passion, Neal was concerned only with her gnawing hunger for fulfillment. All she wanted was appeasement. She had to have him; she meant to have him. This time she wouldn't retreat, and she wouldn't let him if he tried to.

"Neal," he had whispered in a fevered moment of their passion, "I love you, and I've got to have you."

"I love you," she had confessed joyously, not knowing that her happiness was to be so short-lived, not understanding Edric's concept of love.

Then he had lifted her into his arms and had carried her into the house, where he laid her on the bed in the front bedroom. He gave her time to change her mind, time to think about the consequences of their desirous overtures. Quietly he moved through the house, locking the door, making sure they wouldn't be disturbed. If she really wanted him, their time together wouldn't be interrupted and ruined because of an oversight on his part.

He returned to the bedroom and looked at the soft vision on the bed. At that moment—that precise moment —Edric did love her. But he didn't equate love with commitment or endurance. To him it was synonymous with want, need, and take. It wasn't until he'd lost Neal that he began to reevaluate his life-style. By then, however, it was too late. After that he became even less caring and more demanding of the woman, giving less and less of himself.

He sat down on the edge of the bed, and his fingers slipped under the purple strap. He pulled it once, and the strap gave. He lifted his feet and swung them on the bed at the same time that he tugged the top, and her breasts spilled free. As Edric's brown eyes devoured them, his fingers carefully touched the satin skin, moving around the areola first, then brushing against the nipple, watching it spring into life.

Hotly his eyes caressed her as his hand continued their expert manipulation, kneading her breasts into a surging oneness. Then his mouth joined in the assault, his lips closing over the aching peaks, sucking them gently, drinking of their honeyed dew.

Neal's face thrashed from side to side as she wriggled with the passion that racked her body; her legs entwined with his, her hands wrapping around Edric, her fingers raking his back. Each gentle tug of his mouth sent a shaft of want piercing through her, poignantly reminding her of her emptiness.

Her hands clasped his face, and needing him, she drew his lips to hers, her mouth hungry for the warmth of his, for the thrust of his tongue. His lips met hers, and her body arched against him as she demanded his love. His hands moved from her shoulders, down her back, across the tender slope of her midsection, to the dark triangle that lay between her thighs.

"Is it good, sweetheart?" he murmured huskily, his lips moving against hers, their breath warmly mingling.

"It's more than wonderful," she gasped in a hoarse voice. "More wonderful than you told me it would be."

He laughed, the sound jubilant, as he shifted his body, as he shifted her body. "It's nothing to what it's going to be like, little one. Just wait."

Then he caught her hand and guided it to his bathing suit, which was bulging with his passion, and he laid her hand on the moist skin of his lower stomach.

"Touch me, darling," he commanded softly. "Please touch me."

Tentatively her hand moved on his stomach, and she felt him convulse against her. Again she moved her fingers, letting them shyly slip under the band of the swimsuit. When she touched the fine line of hair, she heard him sigh his pleasure. Boldly then her fingers twisted, catching

56

the material of the trunks, shoving them down Edric's thighs.

He levered slightly, helping her with the task, watching as her eyes, for the first time, viewed his masculinity. The red color washed her cheeks, but she didn't lower her head in coy embarrassment. Rather, she lifted her face to his and lightly brushed his lips with hers.

"I love you." The soft confession escaped her mouth. "You're so wonderful and so beautiful, Edric."

Edric had clasped her closely to him, freely taking of her goodness, letting it seep into his flesh, his bones, his marrow. His hands moved up and down her back, and he felt the warmth of her breasts as they crushed his chest. When her hands traveled from his face, to his abdomen, to the center of his burgeoning masculinity, Edric gasped. Lovingly he prepared her for entry, and his lips captured hers in a long, drugging kiss. Gently he levered himself over her.

"I thought I'd find you here."

The quiet words broke into Neal's dreams, and she looked up at Edric, her eyes shimmering with stars. She smiled at him dreamily and ran her hands through the short curls that framed her face. Then she lifted her hand and slid her feet up.

"Help me up, please."

He caught the hand and pulled her up with such force that she would have fallen against him if she hadn't quickly thrown her hands between his body and hers.

He cocked his brows in question. "No?"

She shook her head. "No."

"Weren't you thinking about this when you were sitting here?" he asked, almost positive that she had been remembering that day so long ago, wondering if it had been as precious to her as it had become to him.

She smiled. "To be truthful"—she paused, devilish mischief prompting her to hesitate, to make him wonder—"I *was* thinking about you and me."

"And our special day," he finished.

As intently as she stared at him, Edric stared into her face, a chary glint in his eyes. He hadn't figured Neal out yet. He couldn't understand her truthful directness. Most women, when playing the game of seductive dangling, didn't use this weapon. Was she attracted to him, or was she trying to prove something to herself? If so, what? He didn't know which, and it bothered him.

"Was it special to you?" he asked with the same blunt directness, deciding that the only way to fight fire was with fire.

Her eyes were beautiful, unusually so. From the center of the iris the color splintered out, going from deep blue to purple, and the purple deepened, forming a dark ring around the circle of blue. Even now he could still see the starry images of the past as they gracefully danced in the dreamy depths.

"Yes." The soft sound whispered to him, caressing his ears. "It was very special to me, and I was remembering it."

One arm circled her loosely, and his hand rested against her lower back. The other hand still held her hand. He knew that at this moment she was his for the taking, and he knew that it was because of her memories. At the same time her candor puzzled him, but it didn't daunt him. He lowered his head.

She shook her head, lightly pushing her hands against his chest, moving away from his touch. "No, Edric, not now." She paused; then she explained in low tones. "I must have time." Her eyes earnestly sought his. "Mom would cringe if she could hear me say this, but I'm trying to find myself." She laughed; again the soft, musical tones were caressively sweet to Edric's frayed emotions. "I came

58

to find out if I was over my puppy love before I contacted Kerry to give him my answer."

"And are you?" he asked, not sure that he wanted to hear her answer. He wasn't sure that he was really ready for her answer.

The smile lingered in her eyes and on her lips; she nodded. "I think so."

Edric's hand went to the brim of his hat, and he flicked it forward, lower on the forehead. His features were tight and set, his chin jutting out. There was no answering smile in his eyes or on his mouth.

"I don't think so." With whiplike precision the words cracked through the air. "No, Neal Freeman, I don't think you're over your puppy love," he declared. He turned on his heels and walked back to the house. He stopped to wait for her when he reached the cedar arbor. "Duncan and the others have gone. I guess we'll go on to the house for supper. Are you ready?"

Neal looked into the strong, angular face, and she nodded. "I'm ready." And when he held out his large, calloused hand, she dropped her smaller one into it.

Suddenly she felt lighter than she had for a long time, and she began to hum, not realizing the tune was about thirteen years old, not thinking about its being one of her favorite songs when she and Edric were dating.

Neal didn't look up, so she didn't see the joy that splashed on Edric's face. She didn't see the gentle smile that tugged at the strong, firm lips; she didn't see the tender delight that sparkled in those tawny eyes. Rather, she was deep in her own thoughts, a secret smile curving her lips.

She hadn't lied to Edric. She was over her puppy love. But she'd discovered something else, something she didn't tell him about, something she might possibly never tell him. She wanted him more now than she had wanted him when she was younger. Perhaps she was still in love with him, but if that was so, it was a distinctly different kind of love. Maturity brought with it a deeper understanding, a deeper need and desire.

Rousing from his thoughts, rousing her from her thoughts, Edric said, "Ready to go home, Neal?"

She never consciously noticed his choice of words because they sounded right to her heart. "Yes." She sighed, glancing over her shoulder for one last look at the sinking sun and the lovely evening shadows which descended on the old willow tree. "I'm ready to go home."

She never noticed her use of the word, but Edric did.

CHAPTER THREE

As soon as Sam and his wife, Livy, disappeared into the covey of people who were making their way to the dance floor, Neal scooted across the smoothly finished log bench and leaned against the wall of the huge dance hall. Sipping her beer, she slowly relaxed to the soothing beat of the country and western music. Unlike many singles who frequented the Bucking Bronc, Neal didn't mind sitting by herself. In fact, she preferred it. She was not an avid dancer but was one of those who would dance occasionally to placate her escort. Neal much preferred to be a spectator, welcoming the chance to sit alone and silently observe her surroundings.

For a while her eyes followed the movements of Sam and Livy, but finally tiring of that, she allowed her gaze to flick indiscriminately from the dancers to the people who were huddled around the tables. Some were talking loudly and boisterously; others were quietly eating their dinners. Still others, mostly couples, were sitting close together, whispering secrets and nuzzling one another.

Then Neal's face lifted, and she gazed at the bar across the room, her eyes leisurely moving from one person to the next as she studied each. Her eyes stopped when she encountered that familiar face, the one she invariably sought out of any crowd. Was she surprised? No, she thought, not really, calmly accepting his presence. She had known that they would meet again sooner or later.

Evidently Edric had been watching her for a good while, yet he made no effort to acknowledge that he saw her. He just continued to stare. His lips didn't curve into an answering smile; he didn't lift his hand to wave; he didn't even nod. Rather, he gazed, drinking his fill of her beauty.

Without a trace of embarrassment, without mental censure Neal returned his stare. She allowed herself to drink in his rugged handsomeness, steeped herself in the blatant masculinity that his presence exuded. Voraciously her eyes roamed over the thick, shining hair that fell softly over his forehead, the golden brown eyes that were seriously studying her, the lips that were slightly parted. She loved the chiseled facial features that could so quickly be softened by tenderness.

She remembered the feel of that thick, muscular neck that veed into the dark green shirt, and she wanted to stroke the broad shoulders that rippled under the silky stretch of the fabric. She wanted to feel the crisp wiriness of the dark hair against her lips as she searched for the twin pleasure points on his chest. She wanted to feel the warmth of his body next to hers.

Her gaze lowered to encounter those hands that lay idly on the counter, the fingers of one loosely wrapped around his beer mug, the other playing with a book of matches. From the distance Neal couldn't see the fingers, but she could remember the calloused feel of them on her skin. And as her body began to respond to these remembered sensations, her tongue enameled her lips with a moistened sheen; then her teeth teased the lower lip by gently catching the soft fullness and holding it captive.

Edric, conscious of the effect he was having on Neal, deliberately lifted the mug to his lips and drained it of the

62

amber liquid. All the while, however, his eyes never left her face; rather, the brooding eyes did their best to evoke sensual memories, daring her to remember past pleasures, willing her to envision new delights.

The eloquent message of his eyes, a message laden with delightful promises, totally captured Neal's imagination, enchanted her, overwhelmed her. She didn't concern herself with deeper meanings; she didn't delve into the mystical realm of love, or responsibility, or commitment. She accepted, and honestly so, that she and Edric were attracted to each other. Just that and no more!

Accepting that, she could accept that this evening might be the only one he would offer her, but she wanted that much. Ever since she'd seen him that afternoon three weeks before, her body, her senses, her needs, had been reawakened. The embers of desire had been fanned into a low fire that burned in her bones, that charred the marrow of her being, going beyond the superficial, reaching to the depths of Neal's soul. And with no question, with no doubt, with no hesitancy, she knew she would take whatever Edric offered. As much. As little.

At last Edric stood. He moved from the bar, lithely walking down the two steps, closing the distance between him and Neal, his eyes locked with hers, denying her visual access to anything else but him. He, too, recognized the instinctive sexual desideration that existed between the two of them, and like her, he would accept whatever she offered. Unlike her, though, he wouldn't accept less, and he would press for more; he would demand more.

He didn't ask if he could join her; she didn't entertain the idea of refusing him. Again there was no question nor doubt in her mind. She didn't even wonder why he was there. She knew. He had wanted to be with her as much as she wanted to be with him. He had hunted her up; he'd found her. Was this conceit speaking? No, just that deep-seated truth and revelation that come with heartfelt relationships.

The long legs, covered with the spread of expensive denim, swung over the bench, not across from her, but beside her, and he slid close, pushing her farther into the corner. Because his back was to the light, his face was shadowed, but Neal could see the twinkling glints in the dark circle of brown, and she could see the parted lips that now curved into a smile. Her shallow breathing caused her breasts to lift and fall beneath the soft cotton of her shirt.

Edric gazed into her face, noting that same wanting in her eyes that had haunted him for the past few weeks. With perverse satisfaction he recognized that she was as sexually indigent as he.

Edric also recognized that Neal, like him, was seeking a deeper and fuller meaning to life. But this thought didn't surface to complete awareness for Edric; it lay, rather, on the outer fringes of conscious thought, a constant nagging. At the moment he was more interested in reacquainting himself and his body with Neal, learning her, tasting her, feeling her, enjoying her. Later he would dig deeper than superficial attraction; later he would understand the special insight he alone had into this woman. How they seemed instinctively to know and understand each other.

He was glad when he saw the welcoming smile in her eyes; he was glad that he had come. And his coming hadn't been coincidental; it was a planned action on his part. He had known that Neal was carefully avoiding him, and he hadn't thwarted her plans. But at the same time he had been carefully laying his. When he had learned from Sam earlier in the week that Neal accompanied them every Friday night to the Bucking Bronc, he executed his first move. He hadn't known whether she would have a date or not; he hadn't cared. That was a small obstacle that he could easily hurdle.

Neither spoke for a few minutes after Edric sat down. Neal continued to sip her drink and watch the dancers. Edric, both arms resting on the tabletop, watched Neal, an enigmatic smile hovering on his full, firm lips. When the music had stopped, however, Edric moved, lowering his head, his lips touching the short curls that covered Neal's ears.

"What are you going to do now?" he whispered.

Neal glanced sideways at him, lifting her brows. She knew what he meant, but she wouldn't admit it. "What do you mean?"

He grinned. "I mean, what are you going to look at now that the song is over?"

Her eyes rollicked with an answering smile seconds before her lips curved and the rich sound of a chuckle gurgled out. "Are you jealous?"

"Yes," he succinctly replied. "I'm jealous of anything that takes your interest and attention away from me." His words were soft, but Neal could hear the truth that threaded through them. His confession tasted sweet to her soul, and she swallowed a mouthful of air, trying to still her erratic heartbeat.

Keeping his eyes on Sam and Livy as they progressed slowly through the crowd of people, Edric asked, "What have you been doing with yourself?" With satisfaction he saw the older couple sit at another table with friends.

Neal shrugged, her fingers tracing the outline of the red and white squares on the tablecloth. "Not much. Working mostly."

"How come you waited until you knew I wouldn't be home to return Molly's dress?"

"I didn't," Neal said evasively, her eyes glued to the table where Sam and Livy were sitting. Then she felt Edric's incredulity. "At least, I didn't do it intentionally," she amended feebly.

She wished Sam and Livy hadn't abandoned her like this; she needed their support. Now that Edric was so close, now that he was here beside her, she was suddenly apprehensive. Suddenly she had second thoughts.

"No?" The low guttural sound eloquently portrayed his skepticism. "They're not coming back right now, you know," he observed in a matter-of-fact tone. His eyes fluttered back to Sam and Livy before they lit on the woman sitting next to him. "They'll stay with the Johnsons until the next dance at least. Maybe longer."

Neal turned her head slowly, the large blue-violet eyes meeting the amused golden brown ones. She lifted her mug and took another drink of the beer, swallowing at leisure, assuming an indifference that she was far from feeling.

"What makes you think I care if they come back at all?"

Edric's smile widened as he effortlessly shifted his weight on the bench and his hand caught Neal's mug. He ever so quickly took it out of her hand and set it on the table. Neal's eyes opened wider, and, shocked, she stared into his face.

Again he spoke in soft, controlled tones, his voice just loud enough for Neal to hear. "Look, Neal, we were doing better the other day. None of this coy, evasive bit! No more lies! Let's swing back to the truth. Okay? I think both of us can handle that much better." The tawny orbs flashed with direct accusation. "I don't have time to be bothered with such trivia."

Mimicking Edric's tone, Neal returned childishly, "And perhaps I don't have time to be bothered with you." She couldn't tolerate his haughty arrogance at her expense. "I didn't ask you to come sit with me."

"Neal." The soft-spoken word, caressingly sweet, was a plea, a heartfelt plea. "Please." His thumb began to stroke her chin, never coming any higher than the bottom line of

66

her lower lip. "I wouldn't have come if you hadn't given the invitation." He wasn't speaking arrogantly; he was stating a fact, plain and simple. "Your eyes," he said, visually caressing each feature as he spoke, "your face, your entire body. All of you was asking me to be closer to you."

His touch and the bittersweetness in his voice were her total undoing. An eruption of emotions robbed her of all coherent thought, and she succumbed to the onslaught. After all, she reasoned, dispelling her apprehension with as much ease as she could slip out of an unwanted garment, this is what I want. Why be hypocritical? Like Edric, I don't have time for foolishness. Furthermore, she asked herself, what's wrong with my taking what I want?

"Remember," he reminded her in that same caressive thrum, "you said you're no longer a child, so quit acting like one."

She licked her lips, her eyes never leaving his face, and she nodded. "You're right." She paused. Her heartbeat accelerated when that tender smile quirked those firm lips. "How did you know that I'd be here?" Her question was breathy and soft.

"Sam told me earlier when I called."

"He"—Neal hadn't felt this happy for a long time; she hadn't felt this carefree since the day she'd found Edric with Alexa—"didn't tell me that you were coming."

"He didn't know," Edric pointed out. "I called him about the buffaloes, not you." He chuckled when she grimaced at him. "I learned a long time ago not to confide in either Duncan or Sam if I didn't want the entire countryside to know my business." He stood, his hand sliding to her hand, his fingers firmly wrapping themselves around hers. "Shall we dance?"

She stood, her heart fluttering so erratically and so

loudly that she knew he could hear it. And even if he didn't hear it, she knew he would feel it if they danced.

"It's been a long time."

His husky murmur thrilled her, causing delight to vibrate through her slender frame. Yet she hesitated. She had to tell him. Being coy was one thing; being deceitful was another.

"I'm going to marry Kerry."

She felt his fingers as they tightened around her hand, and she watched the flicker of interest that darted through his eyes. She saw the thinning of his mouth; she saw the facial muscles as he clenched his jaws.

"I'm not asking you to marry me," he finally said gratingly on bated breath. "And I'm not asking you to go to bed with me." Although veiled, the tones were harshly direct. "I just asked you to dance." Clearly he was irritated. "Yes or no?"

Neal swallowed the tight lump in her throat; she swallowed her disappointment. What had she expected? She really didn't know. Maybe she had wanted him to ask her to marry him. Maybe she had wanted him to whisk her off to his bed. Certainly she hadn't wanted him to accept her assertion complacently.

"Well?"

She nodded.

"Come on then." The words were almost a smothered imprecation.

"I'm still not a very good dancer," she said in excuse, following him to the dance floor, listening to the melancholy lilt of the melody.

Her words, however, were lost as the waves of music drowned them out, and Edric didn't seem to be interested. He turned, and she was in his arms, giving herself up to the music, allowing herself to respond to his nearness. Her cheek soon rested against his shoulder, and her arms wrapped around him as they slowly moved over the hard-wood floor. She closed her eyes, savoring the beauty of the moment, savoring another delightful experience for her box of memorabilia.

"This feels so good." His susurrant tones flowed like heated lava through her bones, melting her skeletal structure, rendering her pliant and malleable to his will. "This feels so right."

It does feel good, she admitted, moving with him, hearing the haunting lyrics of the song: "Pretend that you still love me." It wasn't difficult for her to follow the dictates of the song as her being flowed into his, fusing them together in a oneness that had never been broken by either time or distance.

It was natural for his arms to be wrapped around her, for his hands to rest on the lower part of her back. It was right for his fingertips to rest just under the waistband of her jeans, gently guiding her, gently reminding her of his possessive touch. Together they moved as two people, but they were one thought, one sensation, one pleasure. Her ear rested on his chest, and she heard their heartbeats synchronize, becoming a part of the oneness, strongly pumping the liquid desire and passion through their unity. Emotion obstructed Neal's clear thinking, and she went even further than the injunctions of the lyrics. She pretended that Edric still loved her; she pretended that he knew she still loved him.

"Have you danced a lot with Kerry?" He purled the words into her ear, only his voice heard above the noisy din around them.

She shook her head, and he felt the movement against his chest. "I haven't danced much since I left."

"Why?"

She shrugged against him, reluctant to admit the truth,

afraid her confession would confirm his suspicions. "Haven't had time," she finally said.

"That's odd," he murmured softly, swinging her to the easy beat of the song. "You used to like to go dancing."

Because it was you, she silently screamed, the words pummeling through her mind. I liked to dance simply because you were my partner. For no other reason!

All she said aloud, however, was: "Once I began college, I didn't have time for many parties." She smiled, dreamily remembering her college days.

Quietly Edric questioned her, and she talked about those bygone days, answering the questions, moving off on comical tangents. Then in the sacred sweetness of the moment she asked him questions, and with no inhibitions he answered.

"You met Tom when you were at college?" Edric finally asked.

He hadn't forgotten any of her confessions, and at times —many times during the past three weeks—he'd found himself jealous of Neal's second love. It was only natural for her to have found someone, he knew, but he still found the thought galling, burning and bitter to him. And he'd been happy earlier in the evening when he'd seen that hunger in her eyes, when he'd felt sure—confident—that Neal hadn't been sleeping around.

"*Umhum,*" she droned, adding nothing to the story. These were precious moments that she was spending with Edric, and she wanted nothing to detract from their specialness. And although she had loved Tom in her own way, she didn't want to discuss him at the moment.

"Neal."

She felt his body tense, and his hands pressed into her back. She felt as if she were a piece of kindling, ignited by the sultry heat of Edric's desires, blazing and flaring into instant flame.

"Spend the night with me."

The command wasn't surprising. She had known from the minute that she laid eyes on him again that Edric would be saying this to her. Also, she had known that she would comply with his wishes. So she couldn't pretend that he'd taken her off guard. She wouldn't pretend about this.

She shook her head, but her answer was slower in coming. "Not tonight."

The two words told Edric all he needed to know, all he wanted to know, and they confirmed what he'd already surmised.

"When?"

The music stopped, and the couples scurried off the dance floor, leaving Edric and Neal alone. Although Neal pulled away from him, Edric didn't let her escape the confines of his arms. His eyes burrowed into her soul, seeking an answer to his question.

"When, Neal?"

She pulled out of his arms altogether and abruptly turned her back to him to walk toward her table, unwilling to answer him. And she refused to look at him because she didn't want him to see the capitulation that resided there. If he looked into her eyes, if he read their message, he would have his answer.

"Hey, take it easy," a mellow voice enjoined when Neal bumped into him.

Hastily and apologetically Neal looked up. "Sorry, Sam," she mumbled, "I—"

"Don't apologize," the older man interjected, holding both hands up in the air in a dismissive gesture. "I'm just wondering why you were running away from the good-looking guy you've seemed to hook." Sam turned and winked into Edric's face. "Seems to me like you oughta be hanging on to him, taking care of him."

71

"Now, Sam," Livy admonished patiently, "leave Neal alone. She can handle her own affairs without your meddling."

"Bollyrot," Sam returned with spirit, "you women can't manage to do a thing without a good man directing you."

Neal smiled weakly at Sam's teasing remarks but refused to join in the gentle banter as they moved toward the table. Rather, she just listened, trying to calm the riotous clamor of emotions that pounded inside her. She was so caught up in her own thoughts that she wasn't aware that the random conversation of the group had turned to the subject of Edric's wild horses until Livy spoke.

"Sam," she began in stern tones, "I don't mind Edric joining us, but I won't have my evening ruined by your talking about those animals all night." Her lips curved into a warm smile, and her eyes were laughing. "Friday night is the only time that I feel we're really alone together. It's the one night of the week that I don't have to wish I had four legs and a tail in order to have your undivided attention. And I don't intend to share it with those critters." She stood, grabbing Sam's hands. "Come on, honey, that's my song. Let's dance."

Sam laughingly grumbled as he stood up, obeying his wife, pulling a face at Edric and Neal. "I think maybe, Livy, that every song is your song when it comes to dancing." His gentle teasing hung suspended in the air, seconds after they were gone.

Edric, a smile lingering on his lips, lifted his brows and looked at Neal. "Care to dance?"

She shook her head. "Too fast. I'd get my feet tangled up and fall flat on my face or my *unhuh*." Neal grinned into Edric's amused face.

He nodded, contented to sit this one out as long as she

was with him. Raising a hand, he motioned for the waitress. "Want another beer?"

She nodded absently, her eyes drifting over the crowd, spying a woman who was frantically pushing through the maze of tables and people, headed toward their table. Is she waving at me? Neal wondered, her head swerving around, seeing if anyone else was returning the woman's gestures. No! Whoever she is, Neal decided, watching her, she's beautiful, and so are her clothes.

Until she laid eyes on this particular woman, Neal had felt dressed for the occasion, jeans, western shirt, and boots, but now, with this vision of elegance coming nearer and nearer to their table, Neal felt rather frumpy.

"Edric!" The dark-haired beauty called as soon as she was within earshot. "Edric Cameron!" Edric's head shot up, and he riveted his eyes on the approaching woman. "Long time, no see," she cried, having reached their table. "How are you doing?" Her glossy red lips were curved into a full smile.

Edric's face creased into a big welcoming smile, and he stood. "Gina Tierney! Of all people! What are you doing here?"

While Gina launched into all the whys and hows of her being here, Neal inspected her, the brown flouncy skirt—not a cheap one by any means—the white eyelet-embroidered petticoat that hung below the hemline, and the expensive cowboy boots. Then the blue-violet eyes swept upward to the wide leather belt, to the sterling silver buckle with its Indian designs, and to the white feminine lace blouse with the fully gathered sleeves.

"Gina, I'd like you to meet an old friend of mine." Edric's voice broke into Neal's studious survey.

Old friend, Neal thought, rallying to Edric's summons, forcing herself through the civilities of the introduction. A polite smile hung on her face, and she uttered the appropriate greeting, put off by Gina's hurried and absent acknowledgment. Her attention was definitely focused on Edric, not Neal, and as soon as she had spoken, she forgot all about Neal.

"How come you're not dancing?" Gina demanded, snapping her fingers and tapping her foot, her body swaying to the beat.

Edric smiled lazily, his somniferous gaze traveling to Neal's curly head, which was lowered. "Neal wanted to sit this one out. She doesn't care that much about dancing."

She can't dance that well, you mean, Neal amended sarcastically to herself.

Neal looked up in disdain. She hated theatrics. "I like to dance," she returned politely, "but I just wanted to sit this one out."

"How about your dancing with me then?" Gina grinned at Edric, tossing her head, throwing her riot of black hair over her shoulder.

Edric smiled, clearly enchanted with Gina's flirtatious overtures, but he declined her invitation. The cool indifference of Neal intrigued him more at the moment. "I'd better stay with Neal to keep her company." His fingers tweaked one of the loose curls. "She might get lonely, and after all," he said, fabricating, "she's my date for the evening."

Gina's long lashes, heavy from mascara, batted provocatively against artificially blushing cheeks, and her blue eyes swept downward. She really saw Neal for the first time.

"Oh, you really wouldn't mind if I borrowed Edric for this dance then, would you?" Gina purred. She laid one of her beautifully manicured hands on Edric's arm, the fingers slender, the nails long and polished.

Would I ever mind, Neal retorted silently, involuntarily glancing at her own hands, which rested on the table.

Most of the time she didn't think about her nails, but tonight, thrown into contrast with such blatant femininity, she came to grips with her deficiencies. Her nails were clean, but they were clipped short. Certainly they weren't delicate and beautiful like Gina's.

"You wouldn't, would you?" Gina persevered, determined to have Edric to herself.

"No," Neal returned smoothly and smugly, "you can't borrow Edric." She looked up, amused at Gina's flabbergasted expression. She grinned even more broadly when she saw Edric flash her a jubilant smile. "I don't own him," she purred sweetly. "Therefore, he's not mine to lend. You'll have to deal with him directly." Her cool gaze swept derisively over Edric's surprised countenance.

A glower quickly replaced his smile. Neal had done this deliberately, he thought. She knew he didn't want to dance with Gina, and she knew that he didn't want to leave her sitting at the table by herself. But, he thought, she's deliberately pushing me, daring me to leave her.

He took Gina's hand in his. "In that case, Gina, I see no reason for sitting this song out." The soundless chuckle whispered through his lips. He'd teach Neal to play games with him. "This band is good, aren't they?" Now it was his turn to sweep defiant eyes over Neal, who sat at the table, both elbows on top, hovering over her glass of beer. What do you think of this? he silently fumed, moving away from her.

Dear God, Neal groaned to herself as she watched the two disappear onto the dance floor, why had she done that? Just one word, and she could have kept him at her side. Her eyes filled with tears, and she blinked several times rapidly. Why had she reacted so childishly again?

But he wouldn't have stayed, a small voice nagged. Remember! He's always been attracted to pretty faces and figures. This isn't the first time that this has happened, is it? No, she answered herself, slowly drawing in a deep gulp of air. This wasn't the first time.

She watched Edric and Gina sway and move to the music; she watched Edric's hands move over her back; she watched Gina's hands possessively curve around the hard planes of Edric's shoulders. Hatred, jealousy, bitterness—all twisted together into a knot in Neal's chest, causing her to suffocate, causing tears to well up in her eyes and spill down her cheeks. She lowered her head and dabbed her face with the backs of her hands. She'd never let Edric know that he had the power to inflict such hurt on her.

After pushing the bench back, she quickly made her way to the women's room and washed her face with cold water. Standing in front of the mirror, she looked at her reflection, thinking that the fluorescent lighting did nothing to hide what she considered imperfections, but what Edric considered natural beauty. In comparison to Gina, she thought dully, I'm dowdy. No wonder Edric preferred other women to me, she concluded. No wonder he still prefers other women to me! With that last distasteful thought she stomped out of the room, letting the door slam behind her.

Strong fingers clamped on her shoulders, whirling her around. "Where have you been?"

Edric was frantic with concern and worry. He didn't know what had happened to Neal. One minute he saw her sitting at the table; the next she was gone. Immediately he had apologized to Gina, had escorted her back to her table, and had begun looking for Neal.

"I said, where have you been?"

The harsh words jarred Neal from her ruminations. Startled, she looked up into Edric's face, which was contorted with rage. Why is he so angry? she wondered.

"I went to powder my nose." She attempted to joke, her eyes wide with apprehension.

76

"You don't wear powder," he returned tersely, grabbing her hand, holding on to it as he pulled her through the maze of people back to their table.

When they were closer, Neal saw that Sam and Livy were sitting there, both looking amused. Sam chuckled as they sat down. "Sure had Edric reeling there for a minute, Neal. He thought you'd taken off."

Neal smiled feebly, shaking her head, but joy was again surging through her being. "Just went to powder my nose."

Still not certain that she hadn't been entertaining the idea of running away, Edric glowered in her direction.

Sam and Livy laughed together, but Neal cast Edric a withering look. "You were so busy with Gina that I didn't think you'd notice."

"Don't think in the future," Edric advised in a grating undertone. "Especially if it concerns you and me. And be informed that I notice everything about you, including your short fingernails."

He saw me, Neal thought. He saw me looking at my nails. Her eyes locked with his, and she wondered how much more he had noticed about her. Then she wondered, What does he want from me? Is this the prelude to a one-night stand? To an affair? Just what is it? Nonplussed, she dropped her eyes, sitting quietly, saying nothing, letting the others carry the brunt of the conversation.

She wasn't consciously aware that several other couples had joined them until Edric leaned over to speak softly into her ear. "Where are you?"

She smiled dreamily, loving the sweetness of the words which were meant for her alone. She turned her face, her cheek brushing up against his face. "I was thinking."

He lifted one of her hands and held it in his larger ones. "About what?"

77

"Nothing really," she said, prevaricating. "Just lots of things in general."

"Shall I tell you what I'm thinking?"

Neal shivered as the breathy question teased her ears.

"I'm thinking how lovely it would be for us to spend the night together."

Neal and Edric were alone; in this vast sea of people they were together on an island. Edric still held one hand captive in both of his, hiding hers from view. With his thumb he began to trace sensuous designs in the softness of her palm. His intention was plain; his course was set.

Pleasure raced hotly through Neal's body, causing bumps to rise on her skin, causing her to shiver with anticipation. Because she had tasted the succulence of love before, had feasted at the table of esctasy, Edric's overtures were most effective. They easily tantalized her memory, coaxing and cajoling the remembrances to her mind.

She began to hunger again for that repleteness that comes with a total giving and receiving. Her body began to hammer for that completeness, that entirety, that wholeness that Edric had given to her before, was promising now. It wasn't as if she'd never been awakened; it wasn't as if she'd never tasted the fruit of love. She had, and now she wanted more.

Holding his hands wouldn't be enough; kissing wouldn't be enough. Dear God, she exclaimed to herself, trying to jerk her hand from his grasp, why was she subjecting herself to this excruciating torment? She couldn't take much more. For her it was all or nothing.

Her gaze was fixed upon Edric's face, and she felt as if the words were flashing for him to read: All or nothing. Did he know what he was doing to her? Did he know that she was hungry for his love? No, she corrected herself. She wasn't hungry. She was starved for his love, for his touch.

He knew. "Let me stay with you?"

Yes, her body begged for appeasement, but her mind quickly and reasonably squelched the din. She couldn't give in to these feelings, she reasoned. She was going to marry Kerry, and she couldn't . . . she wouldn't . . . let Edric possess her body. The wanting and the needing, however, were almost stronger than reason, obstructing her good intentions.

She shook her head, letting him see the conflict that was raging in her heart, in the core of her being. "No."

Though he saw her desire and though he knew that she wanted him, he also recognized the firmness of her answer. She wouldn't be budged from her decision.

"May I take you home?" The words were no more than a sigh.

"No." Her answer was softly gentle but steely sure. "I'll let Sam and Livy take me."

He nodded, dropped her hand, lifted his beer mug, drained it. He hadn't figured on her being so obstinate. He hadn't reckoned on her having become this independent. All he had thought about during the past few weeks was the pliant seventeen-year-old whom he'd held in his arms so many years ago. All he'd remembered was her innocence and her naïveté. All he'd remembered was her willingness to follow him to the ends of the earth.

Now she'd changed, and he didn't like the change. He didn't appreciate her turning him down when he knew that she wanted him. Her eyes, her lips, her body—her entire personage—told him that she wanted him. She was starved for the touch of a man, for the possessive touch of a man. Yet she had the audacity to refuse him, to turn her back on what could and would be an enjoyable evening for both of them. It wasn't as if she were a virgin, he thought, as if she'd never known a man before.

He stood, addressing Sam. "Guess I'll be shoving off."

Sam caught the singular pronoun. "Leaving so soon,"

he murmured, looking at his wristwatch, thinking quickly. Then he looked up and grinned. People would excuse old age for many blunders. "Guess you and Neal have plans of your own for the rest of the evening?"

Edric grinned; he knew Sam too well. "To tell you the truth, Sam, I"—emphasis was placed on the "I"—"did have plans—" "But Neal vetoed them," he would have added if Sam hadn't interrupted.

"That's wonderful," Sam expostulated, not letting Edric complete the sentence, a wide smile creasing his face. "Livy and I are planning to join the Wrights for a game of cards later."

Livy looked surprised, but she didn't contradict Sam.

"Now we won't have to double back to Neal's house."

Neal's visage clearly expressed her irritation, but neither Sam nor Edric paid her any attention. She, however, looked up at Edric, casting him a withering gaze, despising the gloating triumph that reposed on his countenance. At the moment, however, she was too upset to realize that Edric's temporary conquest had been her salvation. Instead of the earth-shattering sensations coursing through her bloodstream, the adrenaline of determination surged through her body. Now she was mistress of her destiny. . . . Well, to be more truthful, she would be mistress of her evening.

Neal smiled. "Okay, Sam, I get the message. I'll ride home with Edric." She looked at the older man and smiled. "See you Monday morning."

Sam grinned and slapped his hands against his legs as he watched the two of them move away from the table. Things couldn't have worked out any better if he had planned the entire evening himself, he thought. He and Livy hadn't planned to go to the Wrights', but why not? He liked the idea of Neal's going home with Edric. Do her some good. She worked too hard and too much. And he had to agree with that age-old proverb: "Too much work and no play makes Jane a very dull girl." Besides, he thought, his eyes on them as they pushed through the door, he didn't like that Baxter fellow anyway. Not that he'd ever met him, but he just didn't like the sound of him.

Edric could feel Neal's tenseness, and he knew that she was irritated, but he didn't care. As long as he had his way, he wasn't overly concerned. Her anger and frustration were just a cloak that covered the passionate desires that raged beneath that cool surface. And he felt that once he'd stripped the cloak away, he could penetrate that flimsy outer texture, penetrating to the warmth and love beneath.

When they reached his truck, he walked to her side and offered to help her in, but she jerked her arm away.

"I can get in by myself, thank you."

She didn't dare let him touch her. She was on tenterhooks as it was, and she had to grip her emotions; she had to keep them under control.

"Your claws are showing, tigress," Edric quipped, a soniferous chuckle following the comment.

"Don't compare me to a cat," she snapped, slamming her door, watching as he walked around the front of the truck.

"Then don't act so catty," he returned when he settled himself behind the steering wheel and closed the door. He shoved the key into the ignition and revved the engine. "You know what that means, don't you, doc?" He raced the motor but didn't move.

"I'm not doc, and no, I don't know what you mean," she said gratingly, burrowing into the door, making sure she didn't sit too close to him.

"Surely now, Neal Freeman," he returned, his voice heavily laced with amusement, "you of all people should know the signs. You're a veterinarian, aren't you?"

"I am a veterinarian, but I don't know what you're talking about," Neal answered with exasperated patience, staring out the window into the dimly lit parking lot.

Edric turned off the engine, slid across the truck seat, pressed his large frame close to hers. "Of course, you do, sweetheart." The purling sweetness flowed over her body, dripping into her heart. She couldn't keep him in abeyance. "When the female feline has found her mate, and I believe that she finds him rather than his finding her, she tells him with her snarls and fierce meows."

He lowered his face, and his lips began softly to nip the nape of her neck, moving up into the hairline, pressing quick kisses along the pathway that his mouth forged. His warm, tangy breath tickled her neck, sending quivers of pleasure up and down her arms. Without lifting his mouth from her skin, he spoke, the movement of his lips bringing the nerve endings to life.

"You know," he continued in the same sensuous whisper, "she pretends to fight, and she caterwauls, but all the while she's waiting for that old tom to see through her little act and to take her."

"I don't like your comparing me to a cat," Neal feebly struck back.

"Then quit acting like one," Edric softly enjoined, his hands sliding up the midriff, turning palms up to cup the weight of her breasts. "Both of us know what we want, and both of us are too old to play tiresome games."

All the while his lips were kissing, and his hands were fondling her breasts, his fingers slipping to the silvered snaps that bound her shirt together in the front. Somehow, she wasn't sure how or when, but she was turned. Or did she turn herself? Whichever it was, she was in his arms, her breasts freed from the confines of her bra and of the cotton shirt.

Edric's lips against the smooth ivory skin sent shivers

of desire bombarding through her, and his breath, hot and thick, oozed like rich honey over the throbbing fullness of her breast. Neal's heart pounded, and her entire body was aflame with that old familiar feeling. She sighed softly and threw her head back, arching her neck and her breasts. Edric nuzzled her bare skin with his searching mouth until finally his lips closed over the peaked nipples.

His lips, his mouth, his tongue, burned against the ivory softness, and he aroused all of her to a new and greater intensity. The fire of their desires grew hotter, the flames almost out of control, as each stoked the blaze with their fevered, caressive hands and mouths. Edric lifted his head, loving the feel of Neal's fingers in his hair, kneading his scalp.

"Can you honestly say you don't want me to spend the night with you?" he asked, his mouth moving against her trembling lips.

She shook her head, feeling his hands as they touched her breasts, pulling them together, pushing the soft mounds, teasing and tormenting her until she thought she would go out of her mind with the wanting.

"I didn't say I didn't want you to," she gasped, searching for coherent thought, for rationality. Her hands, still tangled in his hair, pushed his lips down to her breasts again, and she arched, pressing the surging fullness against his face. At the moment the only reality she knew was Edric and his touch. No one else existed; nothing outside the truck existed.

"I said you couldn't."

His lips continued their frenzied investigation for a few more seconds, but finally her words penetrated the thick barrier of passion around his mind, and he lifted his mouth to speak.

His words were thickly slurred with desire. "And now?"

With the greatest effort she had ever exerted, Neal pushed herself away from him, levering herself up on the seat at the same time, tugging at her bra, at her shirt. She breathed deeply, filling her lungs several times before she began the task of explaining to him—to herself—why she wouldn't allow him to make love to her.

She snapped the front of her shirt, and she jerked on the collar, straightening it, refusing to look at the man who sat alongside her. She tuned out his heavy, ragged breathing; she ignored the wanting that billowed through her lower body.

No, she thought, wishing her hands weren't shaking, wishing the trembling would stop, she couldn't tell him no now. From the very depth of her soul she wanted him. And she knew that there could be no marriage to Kerry. No matter what Edric offered, just a night, a few nights, more, she would take that.

At the same moment that she lifted her eyes, that she opened her mouth to make her confession, she saw the triumph that flared arrogantly in those golden brown eyes. He made no secret of his delight. Vainly Neal searched in the shadowed orbs for more than just desire, but she found nothing else. With a disappointment that she couldn't explain, with a hurt deeper than she would have imagined, she swallowed her words.

Edric never noticed. He was too inebriated with the knowledge that Neal desired him, that she was his for the taking. Humming to himself, knowing it wouldn't be long, he slid across the seat, twisted the key, and revved the engine. They slowly moved out of the crowded parking lot. Overly confident, he hadn't seen the change in Neal's expression; so exhilarated, he hadn't felt her withdrawal. His thoughts centered entirely on his making love to her.

Once he was on the narrow river road winding around the small foothills, he slid his hand across the leather upholstery and closed his fingers around Neal's fist. Easily he unballed her fingers, twining their hands together; then he gently tugged, wanting her closer to him. But she didn't move.

Never would she admit her true feelings to Edric when all he felt for her was lust. She couldn't lay herself open to hurt like that she'd felt the day she'd found Edric and Alexa together. God, she thought, her stomach churning with the painful resurgence of memories, she'd partaken of that one-sided love before. Never again. This time she was fighting for more, holding out for much more.

Edric was a little surprised, but he was still overly confident. He grinned. "Don't sit so far away. I'm afraid of losing you again."

Neal smiled dully, responding to the gentle pull, slipping across the seat. "No," she faintly promised him, "you're not going to lose me again."

He chuckled richly, the rumbling coming from deep within his muscle-corded chest. "Oh, Neal, you're so good for me." He lowered his head, his face and lips nuzzling the silky curls. "I'm so glad you came back home."

Neal lifted her right hand and brushed her fingers through the hair that lay on her temple. She couldn't say the same. She wasn't so sure that she was glad she'd come back home. At the moment she was one big bundle of confusion.

"By the way," Edric added softly, a joyful lilt to his voice, "where do you live? I was headed for your old house." He glanced down at her. "You're not living there, are you?"

She shook her head seconds before she spoke. "No, I don't live there anymore." Her head swerved, and her eyes raked over the darkly shadowed terrain. "We—we sold the house during Christmas break the first year I was away at college."

Edric sensed her sadness and wished he hadn't brought the subject up. "Where do you live?"

"I've rented a small cottage on the river."

"Where'bouts?"

In a low drone she gave him the directions automatically, her mind doing little cogitating on the present, totally immersed in the past. She remembered her last days in the old house before she went to college; she remembered that day when she'd walked up those steps, when she'd opened that door. She thought her life had ended that day. And in a manner of speaking it had; all that was left was simple existence.

Young and naïve, in love, she had begun pressing Edric for marriage. She had assumed that this would be the natural progression of their romance. But it wasn't. Instead, she and Edric began to quarrel, and Edric's visits and calls became less frequent. When they would see each other, Edric was withdrawn and moody. His inattentiveness, his sullen silence, and his long periods of absence irritated Neal, and she would demand explanations and apologies, which Edric wouldn't give. One argument seemed to expand into a second, a third, and more.

Yet Neal couldn't turn him loose. She loved him so much. Just before she left for college, she had driven out to the ranch to see him, hoping they could resolve their differences. Desperation prompted her to shed her pride, giving her a determination to speak to him, compelling her to find him. Nothing would stand in her way; nothing would stop her.

When she learned that he was at the old house, she was glad. This was their special hideaway, their secret place. Here beneath the hanging boughs of the willow tree Edric had proclaimed his love to her, and perhaps here in the same place they could reconcile their differences. Full of high hopes, Neal parked her car next to his truck and sped across the stony lawn, up the wooden steps, into the living room.

Edric, dressed in tight-fitting jeans and a gold western shirt, had been standing in front of the rock fireplace. Neal's bursting into the room caused him to turn around, and his face registered his surprise.

"Neal," he had exclaimed in a low drone, incredulity spicing the monotonous tones, "what are you doing here?"

The blue eyes were sparkling like diamonds, washed with the water of her tears. "Edric," she begged, no pride left, "I love you. I can't stand for us to be like this."

"Like how?" he had asked hollowly, wishing they could have avoided this confrontation.

Caught up in her own misery, Neal didn't notice Edric's lack of exhilaration at her sudden appearance; she wouldn't have cared anyway. "Arguing. Hurting each other. Please let's make up. I want it to be like it was."

Edric shook his head. "It can't be like it was, Neal." The tones were placating and sad. "It's beyond that point."

Neal had heard the finality in his words; she heard the sad good-bye. "This is it?" she had asked, her lips trembling, her words no more than teary sobs. "All we've meant to each other, all that we've shared, it's over?" She unashamedly allowed the tears to trail down her cheeks. "My making love to you . . . nothing! Just—just an affair. No more!" She had gulped, lifting both hands, wiping the tears from her face. "You didn't mean it when you said you loved me? You don't want to marry me?"

"I love you." Had Neal been looking, had she been able to read his amber eyes, she would have seen the grief and sorrow that clouded them. Then he spoke again. "But I don't think marriage is for us."

"Why, Edric?" she had cried, her heart bursting into tiny pieces, exploding into minute particles, spewing despair through her body. "Oh, my God, why not?" She couldn't believe her ears; his words weren't penetrating into conscious cognition. "I love you, and I want to marry you. I want to have your babies." On and on the torrential words and phrases poured out, drowning Edric with the intensity of their grief and growing hysteria.

Gently but firmly, Edric had walked to where she stood, placed a corded fist on each shoulder, shaken her. "I never once talked about marriage, Neal," he slowly emphasized. "I don't want marriage."

Her eyes widened; she couldn't be hearing this. For the past nine months she had lived in a fantasy world, dreaming about her marriage to Edric, thinking about their home, their children, their love.

"You're not serious." She gasped in disbelief. He couldn't mean it. He couldn't!

Although worldly-wise, Edric had never dealt with a situation like this one before. But then, he reminded himself, he'd never before gone with a woman so young and so inexperienced. He didn't know how to extricate himself from the affair and leave her integrity and dignity intact at the same time.

Of course he had loved Neal; still loved her, he admitted, looking down into her tormented face, but he wasn't ready for marriage, and neither was she. But she was too distraught for him to reason with. Still, he had to convince her that it was over, finished, done with. And it looked as if gentle persuasion were not the answer.

"I love you, Neal," he began tentatively, groping his way through the maze of conflicting thoughts that cluttered his mind, sorting them as he went.

Neal's face lit up with hope, but Edric's next words contradicted everything that she was asking for.

"But I don't want marriage, and neither do you." He

had nodded. "Of this I am sure. Neither of us is ready for marriage."

His words acted like a douse of cold water for Neal. Her tears immediately subsided, and she jerked her shoulders free from Edric's grip. She blinked her long, thick eyelashes several times, and she breathed deeply. Finally she nodded. She heard; she understood; she accepted his decision. Without uttering another sound, she straightened her back, held her head erectly, and walked out the door. But she didn't move in the direction of her car. Rather, she made her way to the old tree behind the house.

Underneath the swaying boughs she stood, hidden by the drooping limbs, gazing at the tranquil river that lazily twisted around the large foothills. Last November, when she'd begun dating Edric, no one could have convinced her that their love would end like this, that it would be no more than a casual affair. Her mother had tried, Neal recalled, but she hadn't listened.

Worried about her, Edric had followed. "Are you all right, Neal?"

She heard his question; she heard the vibrations of concern.

"I'm fine," she had returned. "I'm just wondering why you don't want to marry me. Maybe I'm not good enough for the Camerons? Not in their class?"

Her outburst was too much for Edric, and he replied in the same immature vein.

"It has nothing to do with your being in my class," he retaliated, the golden brown eyes flashing angrily. How could she think something like that, much less say it! "It happens to hinge on the fact that you're still a child."

Instantly he regretted his piqued remark. His relationship with Neal had been special; it had been different for him; it had gone deeper. But at the same time he felt that

89

marriage would rob him of his freedom, and he wasn't ready for that commitment yet.

Knowing that Neal wasn't the kind of girl to continue having an affair of this sort, knowing that she wanted marriage, Edric had decided that it would be wise for him to stop seeing her. Ironically, at the same time that he was telling her that he didn't want marriage, he wanted her with every fiber of his being. He just wasn't ready to concede to her terms.

He could see the selfishness of his actions; he could readily admit this to himself. He wanted Neal, but he wanted her on his terms. He wasn't willing to compromise.

"A child," Neal had whispered.

She could have and would have believed any other accusation but this one. Her eyes, purple with rage, cut through Edric's soul.

"Hardly a child," she had said in low, husky tones. "You made sure of that."

He had to agree with her. She was hardly a child, but he wouldn't retract his statement. Anger spurred him even further; impulse guided him.

"I don't want marriage, Neal. Plain and simple! And if I did, I would prefer a more sophisticated woman."

Her tears were gone; she had no more. Her eyes burned and felt gritty, stinging when she blinked. Again she summoned all her strength and commanded her body to retain its posed dignity.

"I hope you find her."

Edric watched as Neal slowly marched across the lawn, hearing the fervent plea that would haunt him in the coming years.

"When you grow up, Neal, why don't you come back?" His words floated with the sad refrain of the breeze as it quiescently blew through the heavily foliaged boughs.

When Neal arrived at her home, she had quietly slipped into her bedroom, seeking refuge in solitude. She had been glad, however, when her mother had penetrated both the physical and the emotional barrier, reaching for the grief-stricken woman who at the moment was no more than a child. She didn't recriminate; she didn't judge; she didn't censure. She just held the sob-racked body in her arms, and she loved.

"Here we are," Edric announced, stopping in front of the small house, turning off the ignition. His voice was still light and happy, anticipation giving the tones a mellow sensuality.

With an airy leap he was out of the truck, pulling Neal behind him; then they were walking up the stone pathway to the porch that spanned the front of the house. Neal unlocked the door, reached her hand inside, and flipped on both the hall and the porch lights at the same moment. She turned to Edric and spoke.

"Good night and thanks for bringing me home."

"Good night!" he echoed in disbelief. He couldn't believe his ears. How could his plans have gone awry? "Just good night?"

Neal nodded, her curls shimmering around her face, a smile curving her lips. "Just good night."

"At least invite me in for a nightcap."

His arrogance had faded away, giving room for question and doubt. What had gone wrong? he wondered. He had been sure, so damn sure. He stepped back, surveying the smiling face in the light that radiated from the muted porch lamp. Maybe that was his mistake, he thought. Maybe he had been overconfident.

"Not tonight."

He heard her promise for tomorrow.

"What happened, Neal, to make you change your mind?" he asked.

Her eyes roamed lovingly over Edric's crestfallen face, and her smile broadened, her eyes twinkled with victory.

"Let's just say that I've grown up."

Edric didn't know her words were a verbalization of her reflections. If he had known, he would have pressed for more; he would have tried to sweep her off her feet. As it was, he slowly walked to the truck, opened the door, and looked over his shoulder just before he levered himself in.

He rolled the window down after he shut the door and poked his head through the aperture. "How about dinner tomorrow evening?"

Neal moved to the edge of the porch and wrapped her arms around one of the columns. "Where and what time?"

"About six," he returned. "You choose the place."

Neal shrugged. "Golden Corral."

He nodded. "Fine with me. See you at six."

CHAPTER FOUR

Neal opened the door and stepped back, letting Edric into the large terrazzo-tiled foyer. As if he'd been there before, intuitively familiar with the house, he followed her into the cozy den that stretched to the left of the house.

"Care for a drink?" she asked easily.

He nodded, his hands slung carelessly on his hips, his gaze indolently spanning the breadth of the room. "Believe I will."

As she moved into the kitchen area, his eyes flitted to her, and he caught each detail—her tight-fitting designer jeans, the new boots, the frilly blouse.

"Strange," he muttered under his breath.

"What's strange?" she asked, opening the freezer compartment of the refrigerator, extracting some ice cubes, which she dropped into the blender. She wondered if he was referring to her.

"This house," he remarked as much to himself as to her, looking at the antiqued-pine finish of the early American furniture.

"In what way?" Neal inquired interestedly, leaving the cubes for the time being, measuring the Scotch into the glass. She spared him only a quick glance, keeping her attention on what she was doing.

"It's odd that a rented house can look so much like the person who rents it."

She grinned and nodded, turning on the blender, crushing the ice, watching him walk through the small cottage. His boots moved surely over the polished tile floor in the foyer, and he stepped into the recessed living room, admiring the warm elegance of the blues and mauves that complemented the rich pine furniture.

The whirring noise stopped, and in a few minutes Neal joined him in the living room, handing him the cocktail glass. "That's why I rented it," she said after she tasted her drink. "I fell in love with it at first sight."

"Any of this yours?" Edric asked, his eyes including the pine hutch and the dining table across the hall.

Neal shook her head. "No, most of my things are stored at Mom's. When I've decided what I'm going to do, I'll get them."

Now the smoked quartz gaze settled on her face, and its direct but silent inquisition racked her nerves. What decision? they mocked. You and I both know you've already made your decision.

Neal squirmed nervously. "Not that I have that much."

Edric smiled inwardly, noticing her adroit sidestepping. He lifted the delicate chilled glass to his lips and sipped the drink. "Good! What is it? Scotch?"

Neal nodded with a secret chuckle. "Rusty Nail," she informed him, leading the way into the den, flopping in one of the large platform rockers, "but I've sorta created my own, so I call it a Rusty Neal."

Edric grinned lazily at her, standing above her, and Neal could see the amorous delight that danced in his eyes. She could feel his caressive touch, and her body shivered at just the thought. He looked at the sofa, then back at her, the suggestive gaze cloaking both of them in sensual intimacy. When she made no effort to move, however, he sat directly across from her in the other rocker, and they sipped on their drinks in silence for a few minutes. But Edric soon picked up a loose thread of their previous conversation.

"You haven't decided yet what you're going to do?"

It was phrased as a question, but Neal knew that it was more an assertion than an inquiry. Looking at him, she shrugged her answer. She could have answered him, but she didn't think this was the time.

"How long will it take you to find out?"

He injected a casual nonchalance into his query, but he was more than casually interested. Last night she had emphatically declared that she planned to marry Kerry. Yet when she agreed to have dinner with him, Edric had hoped.

She lowered the glass from her mouth and daintily rubbed the tip of her tongue along the soft fullness of her lips, licking the Scotch from them. She was in no hurry to answer him. She had done a lot of soul-searching today, and it had confirmed her opinion of last night. She had no alternative but to call Kerry, to let him know that she would be staying in Kerrville, that she would be buying into Sam's practice, and that she would be . . .

She lifted her face, and her eyes, sparkling like a blue star sapphire, rested on the pensive handsomeness of the man sitting across from her. Although there was no more liquor on her lips, she ran her tongue over them again, and she stared at Edric. It seemed as if she couldn't get her fill of the sight of him, of the raw vitality that seemed to flow from him.

The thick fringe of black lashes that hooded Edric's eyes lifted, and he looked at Neal, a small flame burning in the back of those smoky quartz eyes. He searched her face, he searched her eyes, seeking an answer to his question, wondering what she was thinking. What could her prolonged silence mean?

Finally she dropped her eyes and looked into the shattered crystals of ice that floated in the rusty-colored liquor. She shook her head, not ready to let him know her decision yet. Too much was at stake, and too much could change for her to confess at the moment.

"You'd marry Kerry, knowing that you're attracted to another man?" Edric prodded, holding the glass carelessly in one hand. "You'd marry Kerry, knowing that you want to go to bed with me right now?"

Neal summoned a cool smile, which curved her lips. "If I were entertaining the idea of going to bed with another man, I wouldn't be considering marriage to Kerry," she refuted evasively. "But you can't know for sure that I want to go to bed with you."

The blue eyes stared into his, daring him to contradict her statement. Thinking *it is a long way from knowing it,* she thought smugly, a gloating hint gleaming in the deep blue circles.

He smiled, first lifting the glass in the air at her, then lifting it to his lips. As it touched his bottom lip, he said, "You're right. I can't know for sure." He sipped and swallowed, then added, "But I've got this gut feeling."

Neal chuckled, thoroughly enchanted with Edric all over again. This time she enjoyed the chase. Before, she had been too young and too inexperienced to know how to indulge in romantic flirtations, much less enjoy them. She had been too intense, too demanding.

Now as a mature woman she would savor all the delicacies of love. She would taste each individual morsel, and she would feast slowly. Although she knew that she eventually would take whatever Edric offered, she determined to make him want to offer all, not just a part, of himself to her.

"Just a gut feeling?" she asked daringly, not afraid of the consequences of such dangerous dalliance.

If Neal couldn't see the flames of desire leaping in

Edric's eyes, she felt their heat. But trancelike, she voluntarily returned the searing gaze, never once entertaining the thought of backing away. The flames enticed, rather than alarmed, her, and she knowingly moved closer to the fire.

Edric's voice, softly mellow, husky with his sensual desires, seemed to drift across the room, to caress her ears. "Maybe a little lower than the gut feeling, my dear." He enjoyed watching the deep pink flush of exhilaration that colored her face. He felt pleasure when the sparkling white teeth nipped the lower lip, when the tip of her tongue touched the upper one. "I'll tell you something else. You're either lying to yourself or playing a dangerous game."

"Oh?"

Neal's eyes, deeply blue, shadowed with purple highlights, glinted with excitement.

"You're not going to marry Kerry!"

"Oh, no!"

Neal's face softened, and a beautiful smile slowly lifted her lips, a husky melody of laughter filling the room. With ballet gracefulness she stood and moved across the floor to set her glass on the breakfast bar. And for the moment she would keep her face averted, thus keeping her secret safely locked in the privacy of her soul.

Edric could think what he wanted; he could guess and have his suspicions, but only she would know for sure. And at the moment, if Edric could have seen her eyes, a Milky Way of beauty, he would have known that his surmise was correct. The stars of love twinkled brightly.

She heard the whispery shuffle of his boots on the carpet; she heard the soft thud of the glass as it hit the bar; then she felt the warm clasp of his hands as they closed over the rounded curve of her shoulders. His face lowered to that tenderly sensitive area between her shoulders and her neck, and his lips burrowed under the material of her shirt to nuzzle the ivory flesh beneath.

"No comeback?" he asked, his warm breath blowing across her skin, the cool lips softly nipping.

She shivered, her heart flip-flopping erratically, her breathing shallow and light. "*Umhum,*" she soughed, her body slowly moving to his commands. "I have, but I'll save them for later."

"Little liar," he said gently, accusingly, lifting his face, his lips traveling up the slender column, stopping at the base of her ear, his tongue softly lapping at the nerve endings behind and inside. And when she convulsively writhed against him, his hands on her shoulders guided her body closer to the male firmness of his.

"Maybe a liar," she agreed teasingly, "but hardly little."

"That's a matter of opinion," he returned, "or at least it's relative." His lips were in front of the ear, teasing the temple, his breath blowing the short-tendriled curls so that they wisped against her cheeks. "Anyway it's not important," he said dismissively, his hands slowly, surely sliding toward her throbbing breasts.

No, she thought, losing herself in the erotic sweetness of the moment, freely giving herself up to the love that racked her body, it doesn't really matter. She was where she belonged. She was with her man, her lover, her other half. She was with the one who completed her being.

"What is important?" She sighed, her voice ragged with her wanting, her voice gaspy from her shallow breathing.

"You," he said, lifting his face, his hands continuing with their deliberate assault, the palms gently massaging the aching roundness, "and me. That's all that matters. That's all that counts."

Her hands moved up her midriff, covering his hair-roughed backs of his, and she moved her hips in a slow, sensual circular pattern.

Yesterday, today, and tomorrow—all merged into one, and Neal floated from one to the next. Only she and he were important. They were the only ones who counted. Just us, she thought, gently sailing toward a distant beautiful shore, the place where her remembrances, her longings, and her fantasies would become one.

She turned, and his arms slid around her as hers slid around him. She sighed as their lips met in mutual consent, pressing, moving, nibbling, and nipping. But that wasn't enough. Edric's hand lifted to the back of her neck; his palm cupped the roundness of her head, his fingers gripped into her scalp, tangling in the thickness of her curls.

His lips invaded her very soul, followed by the exploration of his sweetly rough tongue, tasting faintly like Scotch. Nothing was missed, no pleasure point denied, as he discovered, as he reestablished, his territory. Gladly she conceded to the victor, proudly becoming his consort through this pleasurable excitement.

She soundlessly moaned her acquiescence, taking from him as well as giving. Avariciously she filled the aching emptiness of her soul, her hands moving over the muscled planes of his body, her hands curving around the broad shoulders. She couldn't move close enough to him; her body demanded more and more.

She had known last night that neither kisses nor hugs would be enough to assuage her appetite or desires. Long starved for Edric's touch, for his possession, she wanted him totally.

Dreamlike, they moved through the doors that separated the den from the only bedroom, but they didn't immediately shed their clothes. Rather, they stretched across the bed together, their hands and their lips softly touching, tentatively wisping across their bodies.

"Neal," Edric whispered somewhere in between all the endearments that had been murmured, "this is so right. This is where I belong." He shoved himself up, propping on one arm, bent at the elbow. His other hand tenderly pushed the thick locks of hair from her temples. "Close to you, making love to you."

Tears of happiness sparkled in her eyes as she devoured his masculine beauty. "I've missed you so much, my darling." The soft words were more than sweet nothings; they were love messages escaping from the coffers of her soul where they had been secreted through the years, protected and cherished.

Worshipfully he bent his head, and his lips whispered from her mouth up her cheeks to the beautiful eyes that glistened like blue diamonds. When the magnitude of her love and happiness was more than she could bear, when it was more than she could share, she closed her eyes, and the tears gently kissed the thick dark lashes that lay on her cheeks.

With reverential movements that are prompted only by love, his lips tasted the salty offerings of her love, her happiness, her totality as a woman. And when she quivered from the onslaught of their emotions, his lips, caressively light, butterfly-soft, touched her lips.

This time there was no assault, no battle for possession. The gentle lover adoringly implored entrance into the mysterious cavern of delight. His lips moved over hers, coaxing them to pout beneath the warm moisture of his, adoringly nipping and nibbling, seriously cajoling them into full response.

His soft moan, his gentle touch were Neal's undoing. Not only did she open her mouth to him, not only did she invite the sweetness of his tongue, but she opened her entire body to him. She opened her soul to him. She moved her body, insinuating it under him, aching for the sheer weight of his body on hers, aching for all the majesty of his love.

Her hands moved to the front of her blouse, and she began to shove the buttons through the small openings. Edric didn't offer to help; rather, he watched, the tawny eyes growing darker with the intensity of his gaze. Unashamedly he feasted on the beauty of the satin skin that was revealed above the lacy bra.

"Dear God, Neal," he whispered, his lips worshiping her skin as they feathered lightly over the creamy swell, "you're more beautiful than I remembered." She felt the tremor that shook his body, and she wrapped her arms around him, drawing him closer to her. "I must have you." The soft longing was murmured into her fevered flesh as he laid his cheek on her breasts. "I must."

One of Neal's hands moved to the nape of his neck, and her fingers burrowed in the luxuriant richness of his hair. She gazed into his face, letting her love shine for him. She couldn't have hidden it from him if she had tried. It coursed through her body, through her being, reflected in her eyes, the mirror of her soul.

And I must have you, she silently added. I must have you because I love you. But when there was no such admission from him, she refrained from verbalizing her confession.

His fingers lovingly pushed the soft fabric of the blouse aside, and he trailed one finger across her flesh, following the lines of her bra over her breasts and up the straps. Then his finger crooked under the nylon strap, and he pulled it over the shoulder, letting both straps dangle down the sides of her arms.

He lifted her body, and she sat up, turning her shoulders so that he could unfasten her bra. He tossed the fluff of

101

material on the side of the bed, and he turned her so that she faced him. Now the tawny eyes were smoldering with desire and fire, their color becoming an even duskier brown.

"Let me kiss you," he murmured, his mouth circling the hardened peaks, his tongue lapping them, sending excruciating shivers of delight through Neal's body.

Convulsively her arms tightened around his body, and the hot shivers of her desire splintered through him, setting him ablaze with a reciprocal wanting—a wanting to give as well as to take. And if Edric had been conscious of any of these feelings, he would have been shocked. Giving in love hadn't been one of his considerations for many years. His primary purpose had been to take, to appease his deep-seated hunger, to assuage his unidentified pain of having lost the only love of his life—Neal.

During the flurry of sensual wrestling, Neal unbuttoned Edric's shirt, and her lips furrowed through the thick swirl of chest hair to find the small points of pleasure. Her mouth covered the masculine delicacy, and her tongue gently, moistly, and warmly ringed the crested peak, and she felt the small tremors that racked his powerful frame.

Without really lifting her lips, she murmured, "I always loved to do this to you, Edric. I loved to feel you writhe in my arms."

Then his hands clamped around her head, his fingers cupping the roundness, and he guided her lips to his lips. With a violent gentleness he pressed her mouth to his, and her lips parted without invocation, without persistent pressure. She allowed him entry into her whole being with that one act, and he graciously but determinedly entered the hallowed sanctuary.

When Neal thought her body could stand no more, when she thought she would literally burn up from the intensity of their love, she unfastened his belt buckle and ran her hands under the band of his jeans, feeling the hidden warmth, finding the crisp hair that shadowed his burgeoning manhood.

Her movements became frantic as she felt his stomach tense with his hurried breathing, her heart beating heavily, the blood pumping through her body. She undressed him; he undressed her, their clothing falling into disregarded heaps on either side of the bed. Neither was conscious of individual movements, of the separation to complete the undressing, of the entangling of their bodies again. They were aware only of the purpose of their actions, conscious only of their desires.

Their coming together as one being was beautifully volatile, erupting into an exploding of brightly colored sparks that shot in all directions around them, descending in flowing embers that glowed dimly. Unlike the many times of his having made love since Neal, Edric knew more than just an evanescent moment of union and oneness. With Neal the union and the oneness were perfect, a blending of two souls as well as two bodies, a blending that surpassed the transitory climax of simple lovemaking.

They lay together, replete at last, peaceful and happy. Neal's cheek nestled against the hard, furry chest, and her eyes were closed. Edric's arms and legs were wrapped around her, and he lay there, his head on the pillow, his eyes also closed.

"Was it good?" he asked, not stopping to think how many times he'd asked that question, not really caring what the answer would be. This time, however, its being good, its being more than sex for her meant more to him than his own pleasure.

"It was beautiful," she replied, punctuating her comment with soft butterfly kisses on his chest. "More beautiful than I had remembered." He felt her lips as they curved into a smile against the hair-roughened texture of his skin. "Was it good for you?"

His arms tightened around her, and he murmured into the silky curls, "It was more than good, baby. It was wonderful." He chuckled, the deep rumbling filtering through the caverns of his chest. "It was so good that I think I must have a second helping."

She giggled. "Right now?"

"Well," he droned, pretending to think about it, pushing himself up, leaning above and over her, "maybe not right now, but surely before the night is over." His hand curved over the shapely hip that rested so close to his legs. "I've always had a weakness for dessert." His hand gently flexed on the soft flesh.

"And what are we going to do in the meantime?" Neal asked, lifting her hands and pushing them through her hair, trying to untangle the riot of curls.

Lazily Edric swung his powerful legs off the bed. "Right now I suggest that we dress and head for the Golden Corral for a little nourishment." His eyes twinkled with devilish imps. "That is, if we intend to feast again tonight."

Neal's face lit up with laughter, her eyes sparkling her joy. "I agree with you." Laughing, she scooted off the bed and into the bathroom. "If we intend to feast again tonight, we should have a good solid meal." Then she was in the shower, letting the warm water cascade over her love-saturated body. Just as she began to dry off, the telephone rang.

"Get that, will you?" she yelled out. "I'm on call tonight."

Edric called something back, and the next thing she heard was the muffled drone of his voice as it drifted into the bedroom from the den. Quickly she dressed, slipping into her jeans and boots. As she was slipping her hand into the sleeve of her blouse, Edric walked into the room.

"You'd probably better wear something less dressy," he informed her in terse words. "You're needed at Andrew Jordan's."

Neal stared at him for a second, ingesting his words. She nodded and spun on her heels, heading for the closet, where she quickly stripped a faded cotton shirt off the hanger. She didn't see the anxiety that clouded the golden brown eyes; she didn't immediately feel the tenseness that tightened Edric's sinewy frame.

"What's wrong?" she asked, shucking her dress boots, reaching for the work-worn pair.

Just about everything, Edric thought, remembering Alexa's husky voice as it poured through the line.

"Jordan's mare Starlight is foaling, and he thinks she's in trouble." Succinctly he gave Neal the necessary information as he dressed. "Do you want something to eat before we drive out?"

Neal, standing in front of the dresser now, ran a brush through her hair. "Probably. Where does Jordan live?"

"Ol' man Dawkins's place," Edric returned, his eyes narrowing on her, wondering if she'd placed Andrew yet.

She only nodded her acknowledgment, her mind again swinging to Edric's question. "There's some tuna salad in the refrigerator. Want to make us some sandwiches?" She tucked her shirt into her jeans, following him into the kitchen.

Edric grinned. "I'll make the sandwiches only if you'll provide the drinks."

"Gladly," Neal replied, rummaging through the cabinets, pulling out plastic bags for the food. "Tea or Pepsi?"

"Pepsi," Edric returned automatically, spreading the salad on the bread. "While I finish these," he instructed,

105

"you can get your medical bag and the drinks and run to the truck. I'll bring these and lock up the house."

Neal smiled. "Thanks."

Edric's slow smile vibrated her heartstrings. "Can't have you gallivanting around the countryside at midnight by yourself, can I?"

Moving ahead of him, Neal chuckled. "This is part of my job after all."

Placing a hand in the middle of her back, Edric prodded her to walk faster. "I didn't say it wasn't," he returned unperturbedly. "I just said I'm not about to let you go traipsing across the country by yourself at midnight."

"And it's not midnight," Neal corrected with saucy impertinence.

"Woman," Edric barked with mock asperity, "get out of the house and into the truck before I decide to keep all these gorgeous sandwiches for myself."

Laughing, Neal skipped out the front door, across the wooden porch, and across the lawn. She couldn't remember when she'd been this lighthearted and happy. She didn't even mind having to go on a night call as long as Edric was with her. She had missed this kind of togetherness; she had missed this kind of companionship.

At best Kerry tolerated her career, and although she knew that she and he could have a marriage of sorts, she knew deep down that the day would come when he would ask her to give up the part of her practice that she enjoyed the most. He wouldn't want her to be on call, and he wouldn't want her tending livestock. He could tolerate the cats and dogs, but any animal larger than those he abhorred.

The slamming of the door as Edric climbed under the steering wheel broke into her thoughts.

"Ready?" he asked, shoving the sandwiches between them, unwrapping one of them for himself.

"Ready." Neal nodded, handing him his drink, reaching for her sandwich.

When they were speeding down the curving country road, Neal, munching contentedly on her sandwich, asked between bites, "Edric, do you mind that I'm a veterinarian?"

Edric swallowed his bite of food and washed it down with a gulp of Pepsi. Slowly he shook his head and looked at her rather strangely.

"No, I don't mind. Should I?"

He wondered what was going on in that mind of hers.

"No, I don't guess so," she murmured.

"Why?"

"No reason," she said evasively, turning her head to look out the window.

"There's bound to be a reason," he countered, sensing a withdrawal.

"I—I just wondered if you minded my caring for livestock, you know, bigger animals."

He answered pragmatically, "Somebody's got to. Why not you?"

Neal nodded her head and chewed on her bite of sandwich. Finally she said, "Some men wouldn't want their wives going out on calls like this."

So that's it, he thought.

"Meaning Kerry?"

"Not necessarily," she mumbled evasively.

"I can't answer for him," came the quiet response.

But you can answer for yourself, Neal prodded silently, sipping on her drink.

"As for me," he said, obeying her silent injunction, "I'm not sure." He laughed dismissively. "But you're not really concerned with my feelings, are you?"

Yes, I am, Neal wanted to scream. I really am. She just

107

shrugged, however, and muttered incoherently, "Not really."

For the next few miles both lapsed into silence, lost in thought. Neal wondered exactly what tonight had meant for Edric. Where would he expect to go from here? She had hoped that he wanted more than an affair because she knew that as much as she cared for him she wouldn't be happy with another affair; she wouldn't accept one . . . would she?

At the same time, almost as if he could read Neal's mind, Edric knew the gist of her thoughts, and he knew what her question had really meant. After having made love to her again, he understood her better, and he knew that basically she hadn't changed. Nor had he! He wasn't ready to commit himself to more than an affair, and she wouldn't commit herself for less than marriage. Evidently they were at a standstill.

His marriage to Alexa had drained him, and the divorce had left him a shell of a human being for months. It wasn't that he loved Alexa; it was that his dreams and ideals about marriage had proved to be no more than a nightmare, a horrible nightmare that seemed to be nonending.

And he wasn't comparing Neal to Alexa. He knew that Neal was different, but he didn't know what he had left to give Neal. Could he be the marriage partner she wanted? Could he be the husband and the father that she was searching for? Could he give her the fidelity that her love demanded? He didn't know! And honestly, at the moment he didn't want to take that kind of chance.

Conversely, he wanted Neal. He knew that his life wouldn't be worth living without her. He knew that he would be only half alive without her. And he knew that he had to come to grips with his selfishness and self-centeredness. This time he must be prepared for a compromise; he must be willing to go that far.

"Edric—"

Neal's voice was soft.

"Where—where are we going from here?"

Edric didn't pretend to misunderstand. "I don't know."
A long pause. A deep sigh. "Where do you want to go?"

This isn't an answer, Neal thought sadly.

"It's not what I want," she explained quietly, only a
hint of wistfulness shading her voice. "It's what you want,
and if you don't know where you want us to go, then I
can't help you."

"You didn't ask me what I wanted, Neal," Edric softly
countered. "You asked me where we were going from
here." To Neal it seemed that he paused forever. "I know
what I want, but I don't know if you're willing to accept
it or not."

Probably not, Neal thought.

"You won't know unless you try me," she said aloud,
reaching for a levity which she didn't feel.

Edric turned off the main highway onto a narrow but
paved road. "I'm—I'm not ready for marriage."

She didn't respond.

"But I want you."

Neal forced herself to chuckle, glad that it was dark,
glad that he couldn't read her pain-racked countenance.
"Still the same old Edric. You want your cake and you
want to eat it, too. Well, Eddy, ol' boy," she said bitterly,
gratingly, "you can't have both."

Edric didn't take offense at her striking gesture in using
that abhorrent nickname. Oddly enough he could understand her anger; strangely he couldn't understand his self-
disgust. Neal was the only woman who'd ever meant anything to him. She was his entire world. Yet he was hesitant
to offer her marriage. He was hesitant to say, "I'd like to
be the only man in your life, Neal. I'd like to be your
husband; I'd like to be the father of your children."

But he didn't have time to analyze his feelings further because Neal said, "This is why I consider marriage to Kerry, Edric. He's willing to marry me, to provide me with a home, to give me his love, to give me the family I want." The tears were just behind her lids, but she forced them back. She even refused to sniff or to wipe her eyes, and when she spoke, her voice was calm. "He's willing to give me all the things you've never been willing to give me." Her melancholy laughter haunted him. "You've never wanted to give me more than sex."

Edric would have liked to refute her statement, yet he found that he couldn't. It was true. He'd taken all the love that Neal had to give. Like a parasite, he had lived on it, thrived on it, but in return had given nothing of himself to her. And even now, thirteen years later, he wanted her on the same conditions. Again he wanted her to make all the concessions, all the changes.

"I wish," she continued, her voice a low, dull sound, "that you'd never pushed yourself back into my life." Even as she said the words, though, she knew that she was lying. She had wanted him; otherwise, she wouldn't have returned to Kerrville. "It would have made things much simpler for me."

"I'm not sorry," Edric snapped, correctly reading between the lines of her words, understanding her better at the moment than she understood herself. "Maybe you'd like life to be simple, but I wouldn't change a thing." He stopped the truck in the middle of the deserted road and turned to her. "Dear God, Neal," he exclaimed, a thread of frustration cording his words together, "you've got to accept that we have something special between us. You can't just pretend that tonight didn't happen. You can't go running back to Kerry's bed as if nothing had happened between us."

"Don't tell me what I can or can't do," she retorted.

110

"I've been living my own life for the past thirteen years, and I've been making all my decisions. I'm fairly competent, and I think I can still handle things well enough."

"It's not decent," Edric charged vehemently, unconsciously wanting her to make the very same commitment that he himself was avoiding. "You're not that type of person."

Neal laughed sardonically. "Thanks for reminding me." Her chin trembled from the great effort she exerted to keep from crying. "I would have sworn that I'd just recently jumped out of bed with you."

"My God, Neal," he growled, "you're making a mountain out of a molehill."

"Well, let me tell you something else, Edric Cameron." She continued with her childish outburst. "I will marry Kerry. At least he loves me, which is more than you can say."

Edric scooted across the slick upholstery. "Oh, baby," he mollified, "I didn't mean to hurt you." He tried to wrap his arms around her, but she threw her hands up and warded him off. "Please," he said supplicatingly, tenderly, "give me a little time. Just a little time, okay?"

"How much time?" she demanded. "Another thirteen years?" She laughed without any mirth. "Shall we wait until I'm forty-three?" Not waiting for an answer, she rushed on. "I'd be old enough to be a grandmother by that time, and I wouldn't even be a mother yet."

"God," he muttered, "you don't give an inch, do you?" He sounded furious.

He couldn't graciously accept anyone's turning him down. As an only child he had always had his way with his family, and as he grew up, he'd learned that being the son of an influential family, he was deferred and catered to. Then adulthood and maturity had brought him more confidence, perhaps overconfidence. His rugged good looks and winning personality caused women to clamor for his attention and favors.

"In a sense, yes." Neal defended herself hotly, not ashamed of her desire to have a home and family, in fact, proud of it.

"Okay," he conceded, breathing slowly and deeply, trying to placate her, realizing he would get nowhere with anger. "I'm sorry. I didn't mean to hurt you, and I didn't mean to get you upset."

Neal shook her head. "I'm not looking for an affair." She gulped shortly. "I've had that before, and I could have had many more of them." Sadly and wistfully she smiled into his face. "I'm at the stage in my life when I'm looking for more. Please," she begged, "don't condemn me, and don't feel sorry for me. At least I know what I want out of life."

Edric sat there and looked at her, only the dim light from the dashboard shining in the cab of the truck, not enough illumination for him to see her face clearly. The quiet dignity of her request, however, pierced him to the very core of his heart.

Neal forced lightness into her voice. "We'd better get going. I'm on call, remember, and you're taking me to the Dawkinses' place."

Edric nodded his head but didn't move all that quickly. Eventually, though, he slid under the wheel and eased the truck into gear. Again they lapsed into silence as Edric steered the truck off the paved road onto a graded dirt road. This time the quietness wasn't comfortable.

Neal asked, "Do I know Andrew Jordan?" in an attempt to get her mind off her personal troubles. "If I remember correctly, ol' man Dawkins died right after Mom and Dad moved from Kerrville."

Her question served to break the silence, but it only added to the tenseness.

112

"Is Jordan one of his relatives?"

Edric shook his head and grunted. He'd been waiting for this ever since they'd left. He had deliberately refrained from giving Neal any more information than had been necessary, and he still hesitated.

"I didn't think so," she murmured. "He had two sons, Carl and Leonard, didn't he?"

Edric nodded.

"Did they sell the place?"

Again he nodded. "Soon after Wilbur died."

"Jordan bought it?" The name conjured up many illusive memories for Neal, memories that troubled her, but she couldn't put a face or identity to them. "Who is Andrew Jordan, Edric?" she asked, frowning. "I don't remember him."

Edric's reply was hesitant. "He's George Stimpson's stepson."

"Alexa's older brother." The exclamation softly whistled through Neal's lips.

"That's right."

Neal sat absolutely still, almost not breathing. She could hardly believe the sounds that bombarded her eardrums; she couldn't believe the message her brain was dispatching. Her first call had sent her into the arms of the one person who could hurt her the worst. Now this call would put her into close proximity with Edric's ex-wife.

She shook her head in disbelief. How could one person get so lucky! In so short a period of time how could she have managed to be thrown into such a predicament as this? But it made no difference, she decided. She had known when she returned to Kerrville that there was a likelihood this would happen.

Neal, she upbraided herself sharply, whom are you kid-

113

ding? When you returned to Kerrville, you knew this would happen. Maybe you thought you had more time. But you never thought of its not happening.

"Horses?" she asked, fidgeting from her uncomfortable thoughts, trying to concentrate on the business at hand.

"Not altogether," Edric returned. "Cattle and horses. Starlight may be his ticket to success. That's why he's not taking any chances with her."

Again they lapsed into silence, and Neal pondered all the ramifications of the situation. Now she wondered why Edric had chosen to accompany her. At first she had believed it was because of his feelings for her; now she didn't know. Had he driven her out for a ulterior motive?

"Is—does—" Neal began, not knowing how to finish.

"Does what?" Edric asked coolly, knowing that Neal was curious about Alexa.

"Does Alexa live with Andrew?"

Edric shook his head. "Not to my knowledge. Last I heard she was living in California."

Neal breathed a little more easily. Still, she wasn't sure. She could sense a hesitancy in Edric's replies, and she felt that he was skirting the questions.

"Did—was Andrew the one who called me?"

This time she didn't imagine Edric's hesitancy or the tautness of his body.

"No."

Without his saying a word she knew.

"Alexa's here, isn't she?"

He nodded. "She's here."

Neal accepted this answer; it was the answer. She no longer wondered why Edric had driven her out here. The reason was all tangled up in Alexa Stimpson. Was Edric trying to prove something to her? Look, Alexa, she could hear him say flauntingly, I've replaced you with someone

114

else. Remember her, Alexa? Remember Neal Freeman?

Or maybe he just wanted an excuse to see Alexa again, Neal thought. Maybe he still loved her. Maybe he wasn't over her. That would account for his not wanting to get married.

"It's not what you're thinking, Neal."

"You don't know what I'm thinking." She retaliated coldly.

"Yes, I do." He sighed. "I didn't come with you so I could see Alexa. If I had wanted to see her, I could have contacted her without any help from you."

"Okay." Neal chuckled curtly, saying nothing else.

"I came because I wanted to be with you."

"Have it your way," she returned shortly.

"Don't play games with me," he shot back angrily. "Either you believe me or you don't."

Neal summoned all the glacial charm that she could muster. "It doesn't really matter one way or the other, Edric."

The truck bounced to a jolting halt in front of the low white frame house that was trimmed in barnyard red.

"What do you mean it doesn't matter?" he growled as he turned the ignition off.

But Neal didn't have time to answer. At that moment the front door opened, the porch light splayed through the darkness, and Alexa raced down the brick sidewalk. In the muted light she could see only the darkened shadows of the people in the truck, and she had no idea that Neal was there.

"Thank God," she cried, her voice heavy with worry and concern, "you're here. Andy thinks he's going to lose the foal. It's a breech birth, and—"

At the truck now, Alexa recognized Edric and she saw Neal. She saw only a woman whom she didn't recognize.

Why had Edric come? she wondered. Who was the woman with him? Where was Sam? Her puzzled eyes flew from Neal's face back to Edric's.

"Where is Sam, and why is she with you?"

La-de-dah, Neal thought, laughter gurgling inside her. Is she in for a big surprise!

Edric opened the door of the truck and climbed out, a smile spanning the rugged handsomeness of his face. "To answer your first question," he returned, amusement thickly coating his words, "she's with me because we have a date tonight. And," he added, thoroughly enjoying himself, "she's with me because she's the veterinarian whom you called."

"I called Sam," Alexa contradicted absently, her eyes roving over that face.

Neal smiled professionally and politely. "I'm on call for Sam."

Alexa ran her hand over her brow, and she tried to place Neal. She nodded her head. "I feel like I should know you."

"You should," Edric said tauntingly. "She's Neal Freeman, remember?" He watched Neal nod as Alexa stared unbelievingly at her.

"Neal Freeman!" Just a hint of sound whispered through Alexa's lips. Her eyes opened wider, and she looked again from Neal to Edric, back from Edric to Neal. "You're Neal Freeman!"

It sounded like a replay, Neal thought, remembering her first meeting with Edric. Her hand curled around the handle, and she opened the door. "That's right," she agreed, "Neal Freeman."

"You're—" Alexa groped for her words. "You're the vet?"

"I am," Neal returned, hating the way Alexa emphasized "vet" almost as much as she imagined that Edric hated the nickname Eddy.

"What—what happened to Sam?"

Neal crunched across the gravel, her booted feet hitting the brick walkway. "I'm his partner, and this is my weekend to work." She candidly stared at both Alexa and Edric, personal crises pushed aside, her only concern for her patient. "Now if you'll show me where Starlight is, I'll be on my way."

Alexa dumbly nodded her head and moved in front of Neal to guide her to the barn. "Follow me," she mumbled softly, preferring to have stayed close to Edric, disliking it when he slowed his steps to walk beside Neal.

"Shall I boil the water and get the towels ready?" he asked, a broad grin splitting his face.

"Boil the water?" Neal repeated dumbfoundedly.

Edric chuckled. "Well, isn't that what the doctor always tells the onlookers to do in the western movies? You know, he always sends the idle but concerned person into the kitchen to fill the pots with water and to put them on the stove to boil."

Neal shook her head in exasperation and chuckled with him. "You're a gander, Edric Cameron!" She teased him affectionately, knowing beyond any shadow of doubt that she loved Edric, knowing that whether her relationship with him developed further, she would never marry Kerry. Not included in the soft banter, Alexa jealously flung her head over her shoulder and glared at the two of them, causing another twitter of laughter to erupt from Neal.

"If I'm the gander," Edric returned lightly, not noticing the interplay between the two women, his head close to Neal's, "will you be my goose?"

Neal never answered aloud, but silently the thought passed through her mind: In a broader sense of the word,

117

Edric Cameron, I am the bigger goose because I love you, and I know that I make myself a beggar where you're concerned. I'm happy to accept *just* the crumbs of your love. Can anyone be more of a simpleton than that? Can they? Tell me.

"We'll see," was all she replied aloud, however.

CHAPTER FIVE

Weary but happy, Neal allowed Edric to tuck her into the cab of the truck, and she snuggled close to him when he slid under the steering wheel. As the miles rolled by, she laid her head on his shoulder and closed her eyes, relaxing, relishing his nearness. She let his strength and presence seep into her exhausted frame, glad of the comfortable silence they shared.

"There's nothing more beautiful," she said with a sigh.

"What?" he asked. "Morning Star?"

Neal chuckled. "No, not Morning Star herself, but the entire birthing process. It's like—" She stopped in the middle of the sentence and bit her lower lip. Thinking about Kerry's response to her prattle, she hesitated to share her feelings with Edric.

Edric's hand tightened around her shoulder, and he pulled her body even closer to his, his fingers gently flexing into her soft, pliant flesh. "It's like what, baby?"

His touch, his gentleness, and his persuasion had a hypnotic effect on her; however, it was really the knowledge that he felt as she did about so many things that caused her to speak. "It's like you're a part of creation, an extension of God or an ambassador of God, carrying on His great handiwork."

Edric smiled, rubbing his cheek against the crown of downy curls. "I'd never thought about it quite like that," he ventured softly, "but I agree. I can see the similarity." He chuckled. "And I'm certain Andrew Jordan feels that way about it."

Neal pushed away from him and peered into his face. "How do you know?"

"By the time we left there and after he and his men had seen the way you handled Starlight, they swore you were an angel of mercy sent from the heavens above."

Neal laughed with him and burrowed down again, finding her warm, cozy spot. "The foal was beautiful, wasn't she?" Then she added after a moment's reflection, "I like the name Morning Star, but that mark on her forehead doesn't look like a star to me. Does it to you?"

Edric chuckled softly, not at all bored with Neal's idle remarks. At the moment he was fairly content with the world. "No, sweetheart, it didn't look like a star to me, but I guess we aren't looking at her through eyes of love like her owners are."

Neal sat there quietly digesting Edric's words, thinking about one phrase in particular: "looking at her through eyes of love." She wondered if Edric Cameron had ever looked—really looked—at anything, especially a woman, through the eyes of love. In turn that made her wonder how Edric saw her. And again that persistent haunting shadowed her mind: What would their relationship mean to Edric? Or how much would their relationship mean to him?

A mature woman, one trained in veterinary medicine, Neal recognized and accepted the biological urges of animals—and of people. At the same time, however, being a woman in love, she knew when lovemaking transcended just the physical. She knew when the coupling was a fusion and integration of two bodies, two souls, two minds, and two spirits. Oh, yes! She knew the difference. And that was what she wanted to share with Edric. True, she had responded naturally, but her response had been guided by the love that flowed from her heart and her soul. All her actions where Edric was concerned were prompted only from the deepest wellspring in her soul.

At the same time Edric, like Neal, was thinking about them. And he wondered if Neal was regretting their love-making earlier in the evening. He knew that it didn't take love to ignite that spark of passion that ran in a woman's veins, and he knew that Neal hadn't seen Kerry in several months. Could her response have been purely carnal desire? Had he just happened to show up at the right place at the right time? Pain shot through him as he thought about it, and his pleasure in their coming together diminished. He wanted more than that. He hoped, he prayed with all his being, that Neal's reaction had been more than lust.

Finally the truck rolled to a halt in front of the small dark river cottage, and Neal slowly uncurled from the protective shield of Edric's body. Yawning and stretching, she said, "Since we didn't really get a proper dinner, why don't you come in, and we'll eat now?" Edric stared at her, and she returned the look point-blank, her eyes never wavering from his. "I'm famished."

Yes, she thought, I know what I'm doing. You asked me to be your goose. Well, that should have gone without saying. She knew he wasn't promising her anything but a few hours of passionate pleasure, a few hours of his company at most. But, God help her, she wanted it. She wanted whatever he was willing to give her. She knew she would take whatever he offered.

Edric wished in that split second that he could read her mind. He wanted to know what she was thinking. "That sounds like a winner," he finally replied, scooping her bag under one arm and sliding across the seat to follow her. After he had shut the door, he dropped an arm around her shoulder to guide her across the lawn, through the house, and into the den. Depositing her things on the nearest occasional table, he asked, "What are you proposing to cook me for dinner?"

Neal laughed. "I just invited you in to eat. I didn't propose to cook anything." Looking down at her soiled clothes, she said, "I've got to take a shower first anyway." Edric nodded his agreement, standing, watching as she moved toward her bedroom, yanking her shirt out of her jeans, unbuttoning it as she walked. "Why don't you fix us something to eat while I bathe?" When she reached the door, she tossed her head, looking back over her shoulder with a playful, challenging glint in her eyes.

Standing there straddle-legged, his hands on his hips, Edric glared at her, a grin twitching his lips. "First I get to make the sandwiches. Now I get to cook the dinner."

Nodding, Neal grinned mischievously. "If you're any good, I might consider hiring you for maid services."

"I'm open for offers," he returned, seriousness underlying his light words. "And I'm multitalented. Maid service is just one of many."

Neal smiled, but she didn't retort. Rather, she leaned against the doorframe and watched Edric stride through the den into the kitchen area. Strange that he—all man, totally masculine—could so easily fit into her small house, that he could don an apron and prepare a meal without losing an shade of that virility.

Shutting the pantry door, he moved to the refrigerator and turned to look in her direction. With a glower he demanded, "By the way, Neal, do you know how to cook? You know, *really* cook?"

Neal pretended to weigh the question. "Well," she finally droned, "I'm pretty good with tuna salad." She held up one finger. "And my TV dinners are legendary throughout the county." The second finger. "Also, I'm quite a wiz with those little plastic pouches that you dump into the boiling water, and—"

"Enough." Edric grimaced. "You don't sound too domesticated to me. Probably spent too much time at the barn."

"At least I have an honest reason for being at the barn," Neal countered. "I have every idea that your visits were behind it and were associated more with pleasure than with business."

Edric chuckled. "I'm told that most country boys get their 'learnin' behind the barn,' but personally I could find better places than that."

"Oh?"

"Under the willow trees, for example."

"How dare you?" Neal flared, flouncing out of the den, Edric's soft laughter following her, a gentle smile tugging the corners of her mouth upward.

She slipped into the bathroom, shed her clothes, and threw them into the clothes hamper. Taking her time, thoroughly enjoying the needed bath, she showered and relaxed. Then as leisurely she put on a pair of shorts and a cotton shirt and padded into the kitchen barefoot.

Stopping at the end of the counter, picking up a stuffed celery stick, and munching noisily on it, she asked, "Is there anything I can do to help?"

"For one thing," Edric said, "leave the celery sticks alone. That's part of our dinner."

"Yes, sir," Neal snapped with military precision. "Anything else, sir?"

Edric grinned. "Since you're quite capable when it comes to fixing drinks, see what you can muster up."

"What are we having?" she asked, picking up the second celery stick.

"I'm warming up the barbecued ribs that I found in the refrigerator, I'm baking some beans, and I'm making a

123

small potato salad." When Neal reached out to take a pickle from his hands, Edric said, "Look! If you're not going to do any more than stand there eating faster than I can cook, then go sit down and watch TV. At the rate you're going, you'll have everything finished before dinner's ready, and I still won't have eaten."

Not the least intimidated by his reprimand, Neal popped another pickle in her mouth and grinned, crunching happily. Then she walked to the stove, lifted the pot lid, and began to stir. "How much longer do you think it'll take?"

"Much longer, if you don't stop meddling." He turned from the counter in time to see her stir the potatoes. Swatting her bottom lightly, he said, "Young woman, I'm cooking this meal, and I'll do the supervising, thank you."

"That hurt," Neal complained, vigorously rubbing her bottom with both hands.

"Keep your hands off my pots and pans, or I'll do something worse," he promised, his eyes twinkling with devilment.

"Don't get so uptight," she grumbled. "I'm not going to mess anything up. And by the way, I happen to be the person who barbecued those ribs in the first place." She walked to the wrought-iron wine rack and picked up two balloon-shaped wine goblets. "I have a bottle of California Zinfandel in the refrigerator. Will that pass inspection?"

Continuing with the same gentle banter, they finished preparing their meal, ate, and then moved into the den. Edric refilled their goblets with wine, turned off the lights, and pulled the drapes open, letting the moonlight spill into the room through the patio doors. Sitting on the sofa, he drew Neal into the cocoon of his arms, and they sat there, periodically talking and lapsing into silence, enjoying the pleasure of each other's presence.

Finally Edric roused himself, glanced at his watch, and

knew that he should be going. But he didn't want to leave. He wanted to stay. A loneliness the likes of which he hadn't experienced since the death of his father washed over him, and he couldn't bear the thought of leaving her. He didn't want to return to an empty house, to an empty bed. He felt as if he were about to lose some part of himself. But he couldn't share these feelings with her either. That would expose too much of himself. These painful thoughts, therefore, he kept to himself, relaying none of his inner duress to Neal.

He lowered his head and kissed her forehead. "Well, Sleeping Beauty," he said teasingly, "it's time for the handsome prince to leave, so he's waking you with the magical kiss."

Neal hadn't been asleep. Instead, she had been lying quietly against his shoulder, wondering what the night held for them, thinking about it, but not thinking about it, letting the question surface, readily buffeting it when it did. Loving the caressive touch of those lips as they whispered across her forehead, she moved, giving Edric silent permission to hold her more closely, giving him permission to love her.

"Tell me, handsome prince," she murmured, lifting her face, which was streaked with the heavenly aura of the moon, "what is a magical kiss?"

His lips placed butterfly kisses on her eyebrows, on her eyes that fluttered closed just as his mouth touched the lids, on her cheeks. "*Umm,*" he thrummed, his lips never stopping their pilfering, moving sensuously as he mouthed his words, "a magical kiss has many dimensions."

Neal's hands curved around the back of his head, and her fingers spread against his scalp, splaying through the thick weight of his hair. She moved into his arms, trying to press herself closer to him; her lips ached for the touch

125

of his mouth, and she wanted to end her maddening torment. She twisted her face, her lips seeking his.

"That doesn't tell me much," she whispered, her voice a soft echo of the passion that welled in her.

Her body trembled madly as Edric's hands joined in the gentle persuasion that his mouth had already begun. He smiled, and the moonlight softened the craggy contours of his face. Still, he didn't answer her in words. Only the sensations created by his lips and his hands offered her any explanations.

"Can—can just any princess experience your magical kiss?" She gasped as his hands slowly but thoroughly explored the gentle planes of her back, as they slipped under the wash-worn cotton of her shirt to touch the naked flesh.

In exquisite delight his lips traveled her face, stopping only when they reached the corner of her mouth. "No, my darling," he assured her, the words springing from the very depth of his soul, "not just any princess."

"Oh," she murmured just before his mouth covered hers, his lips coaxing hers, inviting them to pout beneath his.

His tongue, like a flame, speared into her mouth, touching off any brush fires of longing that hadn't already been ignited. Her eyes closed, and her lips moved against his. She moaned softly, throwing her head back, exposing the graceful curve of her neck, letting the bounty of Edric's kisses spill from her lips to her neck, to the creamy V of skin that topped her shirt.

"A magical kiss," he said huskily, his mouth resting above the top button of her shirt, "can be shared only by a man and a woman who—" He ceased talking, letting his mouth explore again, craving the honeyed sweetness of her skin.

"Who what?" Neal gasped, loving the brush of his lips

126

across her flesh. She knew what word Edric was searching for. She wondered if he did.

"Who have a—a—soul affinity," he explained, not really evading the word "love," but not ready to recognize it yet.

Although he knew his emotions, his opinions, and his ideas were undergoing a quick and violent change, a diametrical change, he couldn't truthfully admit to love yet. Again, if he had analyzed his feelings, he would have been forced to admit that this meeting of souls he felt with Neal transcended any emotion he had ever felt for a woman.

"And you and I have a soul-felt affinity," Neal murmured.

He lifted his head and gazed into her eyes for a suspended moment in time; then a slow smile crept across his face, furrowing his jaws with laughter lines. With tender eyes, with gentle hands he caressed the sweet curves of her cheeks, moving to the chin, his fingers gently tipping her face up to his.

"Yes, my sweet," he admitted, "you and I have a soul-felt affinity. Though we had been separated for thirteen years, our souls instantly recognized each other and rejoiced." His face, shadowed and at the same time glowing with the silvery splinters of moonlight, gazed solemnly into hers. "We may have our differing opinions on what kind of relationship we have and we want, but we *can* and we *will* work them out."

"Can we?" The whispered cry came from her heart. "Can we, Edric?"

His head lowered until his lips rested on the soft curls by her ears. "We can, sweetheart." Her cheek nestled his chest, and she heard the steady thump of his heart. "And we will."

He gathered her closer to him, and she burrowed all the nearer. Reveling in the strong masculinity of his body,

127

Neal moved her fingertips against the hair-roughened skin of his chest. She inhaled the sheer masculine scent of him and submerged herself in the warm, intoxicating experience of being close to this one special man.

He moved himself; he shifted her, and his hand, under her shirt, cupped a breast, teasing the tip with a loving touch. Her senses began to ache with a deep wanting, and reason abandoned her. Giving in to the great waves of longing that washed over her, that flowed through her, she gently caught his hand and stilled the sensuous movement. She shook her head.

"No?" he questioned with a skeptical arch of the brow.

"No," she whispered gently, her fingers pushing the hair off his forehead.

"Why?" he asked, easing himself up, away from her.

She swallowed a deep gulp of air. After what had happened earlier, she thought, she had no explanation for stopping him now, at least no explanation that he would accept or understand. She didn't even understand her denial herself.

"Please, Neal. I need you."

She heard the sweet persuasiveness, and her heart turned somersaults, one after the other, but she managed to lever herself up, to stand. She took a step away from him, the silence thickening.

"Why, baby?"

Edric leaned forward, his hand curving around hers, but he didn't move. Just a little more persuasion, and he could have what he wanted, he thought. He knew that as well as she knew it. Yet he was puzzled. Why had she invited him in if she had no intentions of letting him stay? Why was she putting him off now?

His eyes slitted, chariness glinting in the depths. Maybe Kerry and his promise of marriage meant more to her than he had thought. Maybe he had underestimated the

128

sway of the man and his argument. For a woman who was seeking a family, seeking security, Kerry would be the answer. Yet the thought of Kerry's touching Neal sent hot, raging jealousy pumping through Edric's body. His head hammered with the hatred that he felt; his body throbbed with heated displeasure. Impatiently, almost angrily, he waited for Neal to answer.

She softly confessed, "I don't make it a habit to sleep around." The sweet smile was meant to soften her words. "Until I know what I want—" She didn't complete her sentence. She just shrugged. "Until I've decided, I—we—we shouldn't sleep together."

She had to force herself to say the words because they didn't come from her heart. For the second time in her life she wanted to give herself to Edric. For the second time in her life she would willingly give herself completely without the same commitment from him.

"Really"—she breathed ineffectually—"I'm not that sort of person."

His fingers tightened around hers, and he smiled warmly. "I know. That's what I'm thinking about." She knelt by the sofa, and his other hand worshipfully, reverently, traveled over the sweetness of her face, and he swallowed the lump in his throat. Never had such a wonderful gift been given to him. He had been given a second chance at love! Would his taking the offering desecrate its holiness and its purity? Would his touch mar its beauty?

All it would take would be a few words! Just a few words. If he said them, she would offer him the shelter of her love. Momentarily he thought about pressing his advantage. But he hesitated. He was reluctant to take the gift she would offer and give nothing but a lie in return. Then he honestly searched his heart. Was he willing to offer Neal more than a few hollow words that could be spoken

129

so easily during the heat of passion? Was he willing to give himself to her as freely as she would give herself to him?

He stood, and he pulled her up with him. And if Neal could have seen more than the silvery shadows reflected in his eyes, she would have known that Edric loved her. Only love prompts such soul-searching; only love gives so completely and so unselfishly.

"I don't know if this means much to you," he said, "but I've never shared one of my magical kisses with another woman before."

Neal smiled but said nothing.

"You're the only person."

"I'm glad," she whispered, letting him tug her closer to his taut frame, nestling her soft femininity against the hardness of his masculinity. "I'm very glad."

Holding her in the circle of his arms, his cheek resting on the crown of her silky curls, he asked, "Do you understand what I'm trying to tell you?"

She nodded her head. "I think so."

"I want to stay with you, Neal. I want to become a part of your life." God, he didn't think he could face the bleak emptiness of tomorrow if he lost her. "But"—he moved, ever so slightly, and he peered into her face—"I—I . . . Right now I can't offer you marriage." He didn't add, I'm afraid, Neal. I'm so afraid that I'll fail you.

Momentarily he thought he saw disappointment flicker in her eyes, but she blinked and smiled. She wouldn't let him see her pain; she wouldn't give him that much power over her. She lowered her face, quietly sniffed back the tears that threatened to burst forth, and shoved herself out of his arms. Dear God, Neal, she thought, seething angrily, how long are you going to play his game? Are you willing to accept him on these terms?

"Neal—"

He wondered what she was thinking.

130

She looked up at him. "Yes?"

"I—"

He really didn't know what to say. His mind was too confused with conflicting thoughts and emotions. He wanted Neal; his body hungered for her. But he wasn't sure that she could live with the little he had left to give her. He wasn't sure that she should be willing to accept so little.

Again her hand lifted, and she brushed the hair from his forehead. "I don't think we have a future, Edric. Neither of us is looking for the same thing out of life. And we never have. Not thirteen years ago. Not tonight."

"Maybe we are," Edric contradicted, not willing to let her go, not willing to return to the loneliness of yesterday. "Maybe it'll just take me time."

Neal smiled. "Right now, Edric, I don't feel I've got enough time." Her blue-violet eyes, wide and luminous, fastened on his face. "I can't afford an affair, Edric. I'm playing for keeps."

"Neal." His mouth twisted, a tormented expression gripping his face. Pain-filled golden brown eyes stared into hers for a second that stretched into an eternity. "Neal." His voice was racked with anguish. "Please don't send me away tonight."

Neal couldn't resist the haunting, melancholy plea. She found herself gripped in his pain; she felt his anguish, his torment, his loneliness. All this and more flickered through her eyes, across her countenance. Seeing her submission to his supplication, Edric pulled her into his arms again, his lips searching blindly for hers, meeting them in a hot, searing kiss, one that was driving, pleading, urgent.

Neal closed her eyes, her heart beating at an accelerated tempo as she felt his warm and moist lips planting feverish kisses over her face, her eyes, her cheeks, the tip of her nose, at last her lips. Locking her fingers at the back of his

131

neck, she pressed his lips against hers, needing him as desperately as he needed her.

Finally he drew back, laying his forehead against hers, his wine-scented breath warm and tangy on her face. His hands roved over the sweet curves of her body.

"Please let me stay."

Edric felt the slight inclination of her head, and he breathed deeply. Slowly they both turned and walked into the bedroom. Sitting on the edge of the bed, Edric watched Neal as she flicked off the bathroom light, as she pulled the drape, letting the moonlight dance into the room, casting its silvery sheen on both of them, creating its own magical spell. Mesmerized, he watched her move back to the bed, unbuttoning her shirt with each step.

She pulled the shirt off her shoulders; she dropped it at her feet, and then her hands began to work on the clasp at the waistband of her shorts. She let them fall around her feet. Now she stood, regal and willowy, covered only with fluffs of lace. With graceful movements Neal took those few steps that brought her to the bedside, and she sat down.

"Are you going to undress?" she softly intoned, her fingers touching the craggy face, loving the feel. Her mouth parted, and her face moved closer to his. Steadily, surely, her lips sought the goodness of his.

Without moving, without turning, his hands clasped her shoulders, and his face, his lips, ended her quest. Tenderly they kissed, not arousing passion, just allaying questions and fears. Warmly, softly, they comforted; they soothed.

When he pulled away, he said, "Yes, my darling, I'm going to undress."

Never taking his eyes from her face, he pulled his boots off. He dropped them; he dropped his socks on top of them. He pulled his shirt free from his jeans, and he began to unbutton it.

"Here," Neal said, drawing her feet up on the bed, squirming so that she knelt, "let me help you," and her fingers, tactile and adept, touched each button, slipping it through the hole.

She pushed the material over the shoulders, down the arm, letting the shirt fall to the floor. Then, as her eyes drank in his sheer masculine beauty, her hands, whispery soft, sensuously glided over the massive expanse of his muscular torso, her fingers exploring every inch of the bronzed planes. When he sighed his pleasure, she grew more confident, and her fingers burrowed through the sable mat of chest hair, searching for, finding, the brown nipple.

Hungering for the taste of him, her mouth, following the fiery path of her hands, tenderly and warmly closed over the hardening tip, her tongue swirling around and around. As his body began to respond to her erotic nibbles, her hands continued their total assault, running all over the smoothness of his torso, down the tapering curve to his waist, over the firm, taut thighs.

She would make him love her, she thought, as her body was racked with a new, warm wave of desire. As it washed through her, she planned the many ways in which she would cloak him with her love. She would cover him in such tenderness that she would eventually make him aware of his love for her. She would!

Her hands encountered the waistband of his jeans; she felt that ornate brass buckle on his belt. Clumsily she tried to unclasp it, but she couldn't. She fumbled desperately. She had to get his clothing off him. She wanted nothing— but nothing—between them.

"Here," he said huskily when he saw that she was getting nowhere. He shifted his body, unfastened the jeans, and kicked out of them. "Let me help you."

Then he was naked, pulling her into his arms, his mouth covering the graceful column of her throat with hungry kisses, and his hands slipped the straps of her bra from each shoulder. First he gazed adoringly at the creamy nakedness that was totally revealed as the lace slid down her midriff; then he lovingly fondled the swollen fullness, coaxing, kneading the sensitive areolae so that her nipples peaked in quivering response to his touch.

Slowly he eased her backward, his hands never leaving her breasts, gently massaging them all the time. Neal, caught up in the heat of passion, closed her eyes, writhing her body spasmodically. Her breathing was labored, catching somewhere in her chest cavity, and she trembled all over.

She opened her eyes and, passion-glazed, they stared into Edric's. Her hands framed his face, guiding it lower, arching her body at the same time. Convulsed with wanting, starved for his touch, he laid his head on one of the throbbing mounds. She gasped when she felt his mouth seek the tip, and she moaned softly as she felt hot desire splinter from the core of her being throughout her body. She rocked her hips as he gently nipped, as his lips closed around the budded tip, and he tasted her deeply; he tasted her longingly.

Her hands tenderly massaged his muscle-corded body, down the moist sheen of his back, down to the taper of his lean waist, then to the hard, angular contours of his hips. She felt his body tremble, and he raised his face, resting it in the curve of her shoulder. Her mouth was on his ear, and her lips began to plunder, to explore. Her tongue, one hot, caressive flame, flickered its heat into the crevices of his ear, finding them one and all.

"Oh, God, Neal," he moaned, falling onto his back,

134

"you don't know what you're doing to me." His hand captured hers, and he guided her to the throbbing center of his desire. "Touch me, my darling. Please touch me." Slowly, tentatively her hand followed his insistent, urgent leading, and she touched him. His hands then caught her face, and he brought it to his own, his lips finding hers in a searing, demanding kiss.

"Oh, Neal," he said huskily, his lips moving over her lips, his tongue teasing them. "I'll never have enough of you, darling. Never . . ."

His hips began to rotate with her movements, and he lay back, letting her take him to those lofty planes of sensuous pleasure, that place of utter abandonment. He closed his eyes, and his face gleamed with passion. As Neal watched, she felt the turbulence of his need, and she marveled in her prowess as a woman, a woman capable of bringing her man to this pinnacle of joy.

Her hands stroked; her lips caressed. His pleasure became her pleasure, and she had no thought but to please. Her hands feathered lightly along the inner thigh, up over the tight stomach, down the line of dark hair that thickened densely at the small indentation of his navel, down to the pulsating source of his desire again.

Finally he turned to gather her to him, bringing her face to his, filling her mouth with the conquering thrust of his tongue, filling her with the scorching fervor of his body, shaking her to the core of her being with the turbulence of his need.

"I can't wait, Neal," he gasped when he lifted his mouth from hers. "I can't wait any longer. I must have you now."

"Yes, my darling," she said soothingly, easing her body under the powerful magnificence of his, welcoming the driving thrust of him. She moved her hips against him, with him, and for him, pressing for a more intimate clos ness, searching for that special intimacy that only their love would bring.

Deeply she felt him; deeply the splintering sensations of joy speared through her body. They were one now; they were lovers. It was more than the physical. It was a spiritual coming together, a union of their souls. Soul affinity, Neal thought hazily, her head tossing from side to side. We truly share a union of our souls.

The tumultuous urgency of his desire pushed them toward the summit of their pleasure; the sweet gentleness of Neal's response stoked their mounting tension. Her hands cupped the taut muscle of his buttocks, and she teased them; she kneaded them; she pulled them closer to the softness of her burning flesh.

Then she cried out; she waited . . . one long, suspended second she waited, and she gasped again and again, rolling her head from side to side, her joyous cries dying to soft whimpers of satisfaction. Then she felt him tense. His rhythm broke, he arched, he bore down, and his hands pulled her closer to him, locking their bodies together in the precious moment of exploding.

His ragged and incoherent sighs echoed through the moonlit room, and she cradled the masculine giant in her arms, feeling his lips as they spread soft kisses over her face, her cheeks, her shoulders, her breasts, thanking her for her love. Though he wasn't sure that he could return it in equal measure, he thanked her for the unselfish giving. Together they collapsed, their breathing labored, their bodies covered in the silvery sheen of love.

Later—much later—as Neal curved her naked form around Edric's sleeping frame, she thought, We'll work it out. We have to. But as much as she wrestled with the idea, clung to the hope, she found no solution. Still, she hugged him close to her, refusing to give him up.

Then the answer came! As surely as the golden hues of

the sunrise peeked into her bedroom she had the answer. She would defeat Edric at his own game. She squirmed in her elation, and she chuckled. What was it her mother had always said?

"What's sauce for the goose is sauce for the gander," she murmured, her chuckle deepening into soft laughter. It was time to see if this was a profound proverb or a wornout cliché.

Edric stirred. "What's wrong?" he mumbled sleepily, turning over, wrapping his arms around her, pulling her closer to him.

"Nothing's wrong, sweetheart," she whispered happily. "Everything's all right." Softly she kissed him on the cheek. "Go back to sleep."

"What about the sauce?" he asked.

"Just planning a meal." She soughed quietly. "Thinking about how I'm going to take care of my man."

"That's sweet," he muttered, his lips brushing her forehead in a sleepy caress. "Now sleep, angel."

And she did.

CHAPTER SIX

The ringing of the telephone brought a grumbling Neal out of the shower much sooner than she had planned to be out otherwise. And it was only the thought that it might be Edric calling that prompted such a response. Quickly she pulled the terry-cloth robe around her body and turbaned her wet hair with a towel. As her bare feet padded across the carpet, her eyes darted to the small digital clock on the nightstand. Six thirty!

Is it too early? she thought. No, it could be him. Probably was. He was an early riser. Had to be. The seminars began promptly at eight every morning. So it wasn't impossible. She lifted the receiver to her ear, murmuring, "Hello." The timbre of her voice, husky with sensuous overtones, didn't go unnoticed by her caller.

"Time to get out of that bed, woman."

She thrilled to Edric's resonant greeting. "Edric." She emitted a loving sigh that elicited a quiet chuckle from him. "I hoped it was you."

"Nobody else," he assured her, his voice thick with amusement. "I wanted to see how you were doing and to see if you were still planning to join me for the weekend."

Neal laughed, answering only the first part of his statement, deliberately ignoring the last. "I'm doing just fine. How about you?"

Noticing her omission but not calling attention to it,

Edric chuckled with her, playing the game, marveling at the spontaneous exuberance that bubbled inside him, erupting in joy and laughter. "Missing you and cussing 'cause you didn't come with me last Sunday."

"Oh, Edric"—Neal giggled—"you know why I couldn't come then. I explained it all to you before you left."

"I know," he asserted, then added with soft mimicry, "You were on call Sunday, and you didn't feel that it would be right to ask Sam for a week off since you're so new at the job, and also, it would be unfair to leave Sam by himself." There was no censure in his voice, a definite twinge of regret, but nothing more. "Have you rested up yet?"

Neal blushed becomingly, and although Edric couldn't see the faint flush, he could envision it. Lying on the bed, moving her legs across the quilted bedspread, her body alive, tingling with a resurgence of desire, Neal remembered their turbulent, their gentle, and their volatile loving.

"Well—" She sighed, amusement heavy in the slur.

"I wish you could have been here with me all week, Neal." The thick velvet richness caressed the taut love strings of her soul. "It wouldn't have been nearly so long."

Neal lay across the bed, stretching luxuriously, letting the delicious shivers of passion run the length of her slender frame, reliving each touch, each word, hearing again his pleas for her to accompany him to San Antonio for the seminar. She had wanted to go, but she hadn't.

It would have been easy enough to persuade Sam to let her have the week off, and he would have happily consented to her going. After all, a seminar on exotic and endangered animals of the world would be of interest to both of them. But Neal had deliberately refrained from going. Until she was sure of Edric's intent, she couldn't afford to become too involved in his life. She couldn't afford for him to become too involved in hers.

She chuckled softly, glad that he had missed her. "You've been gone only a week. Besides"—she comforted him judiciously—"you're having a fascinating week—"

"Sure," he interjected dryly, breaking into her sentence, "I'm learning all about the exotic animals of the world." He hesitated before adding in a lowered tone, "And you know what?"

Hearing the caressive teasing in his query, warned of his humorous intent, Neal asked breathlessly, "What?"

"Of all the exotic animals in the world—" Deliberately he stopped. "Of all the exotic animals in the *whole wide world,*" he repeated slowly, emphatically, "I think you're probably the most exotic."

"But you're not sure," Neal countered, shimmers of delight rippling over her body.

"Let's say that I'm almost certain," Edric returned. "I'll admit I've got a little more research to do. . . ."

"How long do you think it'll be before you're sure?" Neal parried, seriousness underlying her question.

"I figure it's going to take me a mighty long time, ma'am."

"I'm glad you told me that I fit into the exotic category," Neal told him softly. "I sorta figured that I would more aptly be classified as a guinea pig."

Edric carefully skirted the subtleties of Neal's accusation. "I've had plenty of guinea pigs in my life, sweetheart, but you certainly don't remind me of any of them. Remember Jethro?"

Then, with laughter and teasing gibes, Edric eased Neal into the nonsensical repartee that lovers have indulged in for ages. Each word, no matter how insignificant, no matter how trite, was like the whispery soft touch of love.

Each, like the dew-kissed petals of a rose, fluttered together, creating a beautiful and fragrant emotional flower.

Their conversation was a guise for that deeper feeling that ran undammed, uncurtailed, through each of them. Their words cloaked the emotion that Neal had already identified and admitted to, the feelings with which Edric still wrestled.

"When will the seminar end?" Neal asked finally when all small talk had expired and their longings and yearnings were foremost in their thoughts.

"It'll probably go through Wednesday."

"Wednesday?" Neal asked reflectively. "Why that long? I thought it would end sometime tomorrow."

"It was to," Edric said, "but Dr. Ted Bryson from South Africa flew in yesterday, and the members of the seminar voted to extend the sessions through next week."

"That means you definitely won't be home for the weekend, then," Neal murmured, "unless the meetings for Saturday and Sunday are canceled."

"Classes all weekend," Edric chimed in, "but that doesn't mean that we can't see one another." He gently prodded her memory. "You can join me down here. Remember, you said you'd think about it."

"I can't," she returned, a faint huskiness tinging her tones.

"I'll drive home this afternoon," he pressed, "pick you up, and we'll have a grand weekend in spite of the conference."

Neal's exuberant chuckle matched his, giving him hope, but that was soon dashed. "That sounds wonderful, Edric, but I'm not coming."

"Why not?" The two words were almost more of a demand than a question.

"I told Sam and Livy that I'd take the calls this weekend, so they can drive to Yoakum to be with Livy's mother on her birthday." At this, though, she told him only half the truth. Before she joined him, she had to be sure that she was willing to accept the kind of relationship that he offered. She had to think her way through it. Nor did she tell him that Kerry was coming for the weekend.

"Why, Neal?" Exasperation coated the words.

"I couldn't turn Sam down," Neal returned. "Livy's mother's old, and they wanted to be with her this weekend."

"I can't believe that's the only reason you're not coming," he stated quietly.

"But that's all the reason that you're getting," Neal retorted lightly, clearly putting an end to the subject. "Now tell me something about the seminar."

Ignoring her spoken directive, Edric refused to change the conversation. "Come on down, Neal. I promise you a wonderful weekend." Remembering the creamy texture of her skin, fevered from love, warmly moist to his mouth and touch, Edric softly spoke his wants and desires. "We've been apart too long, sweetheart, and I've missed touching you, kissing you, loving you." His voice lowered to a seductive whisper that blew cajolingly over Neal's whetted senses. "Most important, I've missed your touching and kissing me."

"Oh, Edric." Neal sighed, agreeing with him, but forcing herself to minimize his sensual declaration. "We've been separated for only a few days. One or two more won't be that bad."

"An hour, a minute, even a second away from you is too long," he countered, wondering why he had allowed so many years to part them.

"For me, too," Neal confessed. Then she heard what sounded like an alarm clock in the background. "What's that?" she asked. "Your alarm?"

"*Umhum,*" he droned.

"Call me and tell me to get out of bed," she shrieked, "when you're not even out. That's a double standard if I ever saw one. Totally unworthy of modern man."

"You're just jealous 'cause you're not here with me," he gibed in return, "aren't you? Wouldn't you like to be here with me right now? Close to my handsome body?"

"Depends," she retorted. "What have you got in mind?"

"Believe me, honey," Edric drawled over a low laugh, "you've hit the nail on the head. It's all in my mind. That's why I want you here with me." Again his voice dripped with caressive promise. "I'm all dressed and waiting for you."

"All dressed or all undressed?" Neal questioned dryly, a smile tugging at her lips.

"I guess 'undressed' is the more correct word," he acquiesced. "Not a stitch." He chuckled when she feigned a gasp of indignation. "Makes you want to be with me all the more, doesn't it?"

"Actually"—Neal cooed with pristine innocence—"I'm not tempted in the least. I'm basically a very modest woman."

"Modest or not, sweetheart, you're a woman, all woman. You don't fool me. Not one little bit. I know what you like, and I know what you want."

"Maybe you just think you do," Neal quipped saucily, "a carry-over from the primitive days of the caveman."

"Primitive, my dear, very primitive, I'll agree." He taunted her gently. "I know that you want me, and you want me in bed beside you." Again the voice dipped low, husky with sensuality. "Tell me truthfully that you don't want to be with me, Neal."

"I wouldn't go that far," she mustered in a small, injured voice, "but—"

She mumbled with that shyness that comes over a

woman when she's intimately talking with the man whom she loves. Not a false or coy shyness, but that vulnerability she feels when she opens her heart in love, not knowing how either her heart or her love with be received or how it will be treated.

"I can see you, baby," he said in vibrant tones, tones that stirred her heartstrings. "I can see every inch of your beautiful body, and it's quivering for my touch, my hands, my lips."

Neal stretched out on the bed, closing her eyes, totally relaxed, listening to the caressive strains of his voice, his image on the panoramic screen of her mind, blocking out all other thoughts and images. She could see the dark hair, combed so that it loosely framed his rugged face. She could see the sweep of the dark thatch that generally waved over part of his forehead. She visualized the movement of his hand as it pushed the errant wave out of his eyes. Then she saw those beautiful eyes, a golden color at the iris, spinning into the dark brown periphery. She could feel the warmth of their penetrating gaze; she could feel the touch of his full lips, firmly tender, warm and moist.

"Oh, God," Edric groaned, forgetting that he needed to dress, forgetting everything but Neal and his need for her. "I don't think I can make it until tonight, honey. I need you here with me." Could that voice become any more sultry with latent passion, throbbing to life, surging with desire? Could that voice lower any more? "I miss you, honey."

Neal wriggled as if he'd touched her physically, and she smiled, tipping her lips with her tongue, spreading a glossy shine over them. She was delighted. Underneath the camouflage of his verbiage perhaps Edric was declaring his love for her. But at the same time Neal heard his anguished cry and knew that it wasn't freely offered yet. Though she was happy with this partial confession, she

144

was desirous of more. However, because it was a start in the right direction and because it promised more, she laughed.

"I'm so glad, Edric Cameron," she gushed emotionally, "that you're as miserable away from me as I am from you."

She heard his guttural growl. "Sweetheart, gloat all you wish. I'm totally, absolutely, completely miserable, and I don't intend to spend another day or night away from you. Oh, Neal, I'm so lonesome." The pained cry made her feel guilty because she wasn't going to meet him in San Antonio, but she didn't plan to change her mind, and she held her silence. "Mark my words," he declared.

"I'm still not convinced that this isn't one-sided." Neal prodded deliberately.

"Oh, God, no!" he exclaimed. "It's definitely not one-sided unless all the want and the need are on my side." Raw hunger rasped in his voice. "Neal," he questioned, "you do care, don't you?"

"Yes," she said assuringly, "I care."

He expelled the air that he had been holding captive in his lungs, but he couldn't say anything else right now. He couldn't verbalize all the conflicting emotions that were warring within his being. He didn't know how to tell her that his soul was lonely, that without her he was incomplete. He couldn't vocalize these deeper, intimate feelings; and unable to handle such personal confessions, he abruptly changed the subject.

"And what about you, love, what are you going to do with your day?"

Neal noticed the diversion, but she didn't question him. She, too, was glad for the change. It wouldn't take much persuasion on his part to wear her feeble resistance down.

"Just work and more work," she returned, turning on

145

her stomach, the robe pulling up, stretching across her buttocks, riding up her thighs.

But Edric, unable to ignore the wave of loneliness that swept over him, returned to his intimate thoughts as quickly as he had fled them. "I'd come home right now, Neal," he confessed, "if I didn't need Bryson's endorsement for my preserve. But he's the difference between make or break. And I just can't leave without it."

"I know," Neal consoled, "and don't worry about it. Another day really isn't that much longer."

"Another day!" Edric exclaimed. "What about today, baby?"

"I'm not coming to San Antonio tonight," she asserted.

"And that's final," he quipped, striving for a levity which he didn't feel. "No mercy for the poor dying man."

"I feel mercy for you," she retorted, trying to keep her tone light, "but I'm not coming. And my decision is final."

"What made you change your mind?" he asked. "You sounded like you wanted to come Wednesday when I called. You sounded like you would come."

"Wednesday, when I talked with you," she explained, "I thought I would come. But I've got to be sure, Edric. You're asking me to live with you and to turn my back on what I'm looking for in a relationship." She paused. "I must be sure."

"That's not it," Edric accused harshly. "Something happened to make you change your mind. I know. You were too sure of yourself Wednesday night."

"And perhaps you were a little too sure of yourself," Neal quipped teasingly, adding, "I just got to thinking, Edric, and I decided that it would be better for us to wait awhile."

"And I can't buy that," he snapped, giving vent to his frustration. "Something happened to change your mind, and I want to know what it was. I demand to know."

"Don't ever speak to me in that tone of voice," Neal quietly but firmly enjoined. "You have no cause to be angry, you've no right to question my motives or actions, and you have no right to make any demands on me."

"By God I am angry," he snarled. "I don't like this game that you're playing with me. It hurts like hell."

"I'm not playing games with you." Neal gently refuted him. "I never promised to come with you. I promised to think about it."

"I want to know what—or possibly who—brought this change about," Edric barked.

"It's not necessarily any particular who or what," Neal countered suavely. "Mostly it's me. Because I love you, I'm considering your proposal of an affair, but I don't intend to let you rush me or push me into a hasty decision."

There was a long, silent moment; then Edric asked, "Have you talked with Kerry recently?"

"Yes."

"When?" The question was curt and laconic.

"He called last night." She answered with the same brisk directness.

"So that's it," he said scathingly. "One phone call from him does it. Tell me, Neal, is he the better lover, or is his offer the better?"

"You're despicable!" she hissed in an undertone. "I must admit, however, that Kerry is making me an honest offer, and he's giving me the best he's got."

"Marriage," Edric mimicked disdainfully.

"No," Neal contradicted, "he's offering me all of himself, and he's giving me honesty. He loves me, and he's wanting us to build a lasting relationship based on respect, trust, and love."

"I don't want you to see him!" The command cracked

147

through the line with the precision of a whip, and it slapped Neal's sensibilities.

Anger slowly welled from deep within her. "I'll see whomever I wish whenever I wish," she quietly asserted. "I'm not a puppet on a string to be dangled or manipulated by anyone. I'll make my own decisions, and I'll choose my friends."

"When you agreed to come down here with me for the weekend," Edric pointed out, none too wisely, "you were agreeing to live with me. And as long as we're living together, I don't want you seeing any other man—Kerry Baxter or otherwise."

"*Just one minute!*" Neal roared, her voice pulsating with the anger that surged through her. "Let's get this straight for all time, and if you can't commit it to memory, then write it down. Maybe—just maybe—my agreeing to think about coming to San Antonio was my agreeing to live with you, but never mistake it for more than that." Although she was lying, she continued her tirade, goaded into retaliatory actions by Edric's high-handed techniques. She wouldn't sit idly by and let him strip her of her womanhood and her integrity without a fight. "We've just shared a bed together, and we've used each other's bodies. That's it, and no more. My having slept with you does not give you the right or the privilege to make any demands on me." She paused; drew a deep breath. I owe it to Kerry to see him in person rather than tell him over the phone that it's all over, she was about to add. Then she thought better of giving Edric that satisfaction.

"And because of loyalty to Kerry, you're refusing to see me," Edric retorted angrily, his heart constricting with the pain of Neal's refusal. "Because of some misguided sense of loyalty, you're spending the weekend with him!"

Hurt but also angry, Neal said, "I'm going to see Kerry tonight, and nothing you say can stop me." Again she paused, drawing a deep breath. For the first time since she'd been back in Kerrville, she saw—really saw—what kind of relationship she and Edric were slipping into. "Even affairs can have dignity," she informed him, her voice cool and even, slightly detached. "I do get the feeling, however, that our relationship is one-sided, Edric. In fact, I'm not even sure that we have a relationship. To me, it seems that you're asking for no more than a liaison—and a shallow one at that. While you're having all your wants and needs fulfilled, I'm doing all the giving, the changing, the compromising, and the committing."

Edric shook his head as if the movement would clear his mind and would stop the barrage of words that Neal was hurling at him. His eyes darted to the hands of the clock, which seemed to be spinning around at twice their regular speed. "Look, Neal," he said, "I just don't want you to see Kerry, that's all. Surely you owe me this much."

"Owe you!" Neal spit out the words. "I don't owe you a thing, Edric Cameron. Not one *damn* thing! And before you start making demands on me, you'd better remember this. Demands are made and kept by people who are committed, and only love can meet the kinds of demands that you're making. When you're ready to love me, then I'll gladly comply with your requests." Angry beyond reason, she blustered, "And when you do decide to love someone, remember you have to trust her. And most of all, Edric Cameron, before you can ask this much of someone else, you must be willing to give it to her in return."

Edric didn't know how to deal with an angry Neal, with a mature Neal, so he began to back off. Her anger had the effect of cooling him off somewhat. "Dear God, Neal," he vociferated heatedly, "I don't like the idea of your seeing Kerry. Can't you understand? Why didn't you tell him that you had plans for this weekend? Why didn't you invite him down some other time?"

"There was no other time," she quietly informed him in stilted tones. "He happens to be driving through from a business trip to El Paso, and it so happens that I want to see him now, Edric. And it so happens that I don't have plans for this weekend."

She didn't bother to tell Edric again that she planned to sever all ties with Kerry and Beaumont. She wouldn't entirely bare her soul for him to see. So far he had wanted to share very little of himself with her, and she would be cautious. The next move would be his.

"When's he coming?"

"About six," she replied.

"I'm still coming home tonight, Neal."

"Not for me," she enjoined firmly.

"I'll be at the house," he continued, as if she hadn't spoken. "If, after Kerry leaves, you've made up your mind about coming with me, call."

"Don't come home tonight," Neal suggested. "Wait for me to call."

"And when will that be?" he asked.

"I'll call tomorrow," she replied.

"Why not tonight?" he asked. "Kerry's not staying all night, is he?"

"Please trust me, Edric," she begged, not answering his question.

"He's staying overnight, isn't he?" Edric raged. "He's not leaving until tomorrow, is he?"

"His staying overnight isn't indicative of anything," she pointed out. "And if you have any feelings for me at all, Edric, you'll trust me to handle this."

"I don't want you to see him, Neal," Edric almost shouted. "Wait for me. We'll see him together."

"No," she replied smoothly, evenly. "I'll see Kerry by myself."

"Dear God, Neal," he returned loudly, "don't be a fool.

You're mine, and I don't intend to share you with anyone. And I'm not going to take the chance on your going to bed with him."

Something in the way Edric said the words gave them a domineering and proprietary ring, and they infuriated Neal. "I belong to no one but myself," she announced, "and what I do with Kerry is my business, not yours." Her voice was icy cold, and Edric could feel the chilly wind of her glacial charm. "And, I might add, there's a possibility that Kerry will stay the entire weekend." He wanted to push her into a corner. Well, she thought, tears running down her cheeks, let him. "It just depends on me." She'd give Edric Cameron something to think about.

Neal had never experienced a silence as heavy and portentous as the one that followed her tirade. Then, when he asked, "You may sleep with him?" she wondered if she'd gone too far, but she didn't hesitate to retort spiritedly.

"That, Edric Cameron, is none of your business!" Her words fell like the sharp, precise blows of a hammer.

"Think about us, Neal." His words had a haunting, melancholy ring. "If you go to bed with him, it's all over between us."

"Without trust we don't have too much anyway," she returned softly, "just sex." She laid the telephone in the cradle after adding, "And I think you *owe* me more than that."

CHAPTER SEVEN

Edric walked into the Bucking Bronc, his handsome face set, looking as if it had been sculpted out of granite, his chin jutting with purpose and determination. With a casual indolence that was deceiving, he stood for a minute, hands on hips, his eyes a tawny gold, surveying the sea of people. Finally he saw her, and a small tender smile tugged at his lips and momentarily softened his face. Then he saw the man sitting across from her, and his eyes turned to flint. His smile faded, and his face was once again hard and cold.

"Howdy, pardner," the young cowgirl drawled, casting him a provocative smile, holding the menus under her arm. "How many's in your party?"

Giving her a brief smile, he said as he brushed past her, "My party's already arrived. I see them over there." Quickly he walked toward Neal, his eyes never leaving the back of her head, not stopping until he reached her table.

"Hello, Neal."

At the sound of his voice Neal twirled around on the bench, her eyes wide with shock, her mouth opened in surprise. "Edric," she murmured in a dry whisper, "what are you doing here? I thought you were out of town."

He smiled down at her. "I told you I'd be back today. Must have slipped your mind." The golden brown eyes, speaking directly to her, emphatically declared his purpose.

Though he smiled and though his greeting was friendly enough, Neal saw beyond the superficial mask of politeness. She saw the flinty resolve that glinted in his eyes. She saw the anger that lapped in the depths, and she felt his controlled tenseness. She sensed his disapproval.

"I'm waiting for Sam and Livy," he explained, his eyes raking over the crowd before they again rested on her, then flicked to Kerry. "I just arrived in town about an hour ago and found that Duncan and Molly had taken off for the weekend without leaving me anything to eat."

"How tragic!" Neal sarcastically murmured. "Poor boy's gonna starve to death."

Edric laughed, not caring that she was perturbed by his appearance. "In time I might," he retorted. "After last weekend you should know that I'm a lousy cook."

Neal stared at him for the longest moment, knowing that he had deliberately set her up, yet she could do nothing about it. Any comeback would emphasize his remark, placing more significance on it than it deserved. When she looked at Kerry, she saw the sky-blue eyes narrow and the facial muscles tighten. His glare, however, didn't crush or intimidate Edric. Calmly he returned Kerry's searching gaze.

Refusing to give Edric the satisfaction of knowing the extent of her anger, Neal in a coolly detached tone said, "Edric, I'd like you to meet Kerry Baxter—" Keeping a polite smile on her face, she went through the formalities of introduction, hardly aware of what the two men said.

Kerry stood to shake hands with Edric, and they engaged in trite, desultory conversation, all the time sizing each other up. As they did so, Neal watched them, realizing that they were a total antithesis. Kerry, tall and broad-shouldered, was blond-haired and blue eyed, reminding her of a stalwart Viking raider, whereas, Edric, although powerfully built, was of medium height, dark and rugged, reminding her of a Scottish chieftain, wild and untamed.

Even in contrast with Kerry, though, Edric dominated the scene, and it was to him that Neal's eyes riveted and bolted. She quickly skimmed over the light-colored hat that hid the dark hair, but she lingered on the beauty of those tawny eyes and the thick sable brows that were quirked in either question or amusement. She loved the tanned roughness of his face, and as her eyes ran along the dark masculine shadow on his firm jaws, she realized that he hadn't taken time to shave.

Lower her eyes went to the soft cotton of the western shirt, the top two snaps unfastened to reveal the edge of dark, curly chest hair. Her fingers itched to touch that firm chest, to feel those crisp curls; then she felt a gnawing desire in the hollow of her stomach; she wanted to touch him all over, to rediscover, to reexplore all the secret places of delight, and to rekindle his fiery passion. Lost in her ruminations, she let her eyes stray farther: the suede jacket, the designer jeans, finally the boots.

Although she heard them talking, she didn't listen to what they said. Rather, she tried to quell the riotous emotions that clamored through her body, robbing her of rational thought, filling her with a suffocating heat of want and need, the selfsame emotion that she condemned in Edric. Composing herself finally, wiping any telltale expressions from her face, she looked up to encounter those golden brown eyes—those eyes which seemed to know what she was going through, those eyes which gleamed with devilish delight, those eyes which locked with hers and refused to let hers go. They commanded her to look beyond the smoldering bed of burned-out coals to the glowing embers of fire underneath, and in the fathomless depths she saw the battle that fiercely raged; she saw the white-hot anger that was barely curbed. She saw the purpose; she saw the steely determination.

What he didn't allow her to see, however, was all the hurt and the confusion that were harbored there, too. He didn't let her know that anguish over the possibility of losing her was tearing his soul into tiny pieces. And he wouldn't let her know that he'd driven like a bat out of hell to Kerrville, spending the better part of the evening hunting her. He hadn't taken the time to bathe or to shave. He'd barely taken the time to change clothes.

Without taking his eyes off Neal, Edric said to Kerry, "Neal's told me quite a bit about you."

"Has she?" Kerry muttered faintly, looking from Edric to Neal, seeing the magnetic locking of their gazes, feeling the loneliness of being excluded from their personal intimacy. Like lovers, he thought, they're reading each other's heart and souls. No words had passed between them, yet so much had been said. His lips twisted into a bitter smile.

"I wish I could say the same, Mr. Cameron," came the dry retort.

Edric's eyes narrowed at the cryptic barb, and he shifted his gaze to Kerry. But he replied easily enough. "Edric, please," he enjoined briskly as he motioned to the waiter and without being invited sat down. "If you don't mind" —his face swiveled quickly to first one, then the other— "I'll just sit here until Sam and Livy arrive." He flashed both of them a big smile that looked friendly, but underneath was a brooding silence, a deadly intent that Neal recognized. Silently he chuckled when she pulled a face at him. "I hate to sit by myself," he softly added.

"Well, we would rather . . ." Kerry began, glancing at Neal, hoping that she would insist on Edric's leaving.

"Good," Edric rejoined quickly, "that's settled. I'll just order me a beer." And he turned to the waiter to give his order without stopping the flow of the conversation. "Don't you like these steaks?" he asked, pointing at Kerry's plate. "Best in the country. Cooked over mesquite wood."

Neal listened as Edric continued his convivial ramblings, and if she hadn't been so upset with his high-handed tactics and his interference, she would have laughed. Too frustrated at the moment, however, to appreciate his down-home charm, she decided that again her best course of retaliation would be to ignore him.

After a while Kerry, also tired of Edric's sociabilities, turned the conversation into a more serious vein. "What kind of ranch do you own?"

Not sure what he was asking, Edric lifted his shoulders in a casual shrug and gave an offhand answer. "Just a ranch," he supplied, "with quite a few four-legged critters running around."

"It's an animal preserve," Neal hastily interjected, furious with Edric's loaded comments and gibes. Completing taking over, she began a loquacious description of the Golden Cam.

When she'd finally finished, Kerry said, "Sounds like it's pretty big."

"So-so," Edric retorted, "but it does have a lot of animals on it."

Kerry's eyes, cold and unrelenting, rested on Edric's face. "Neal makes it sound as if you're one of her best patients."

Edric set his beer mug on the table and began to chuckle. He looked at Neal, and despite her good intentions, she, too, began to laugh with him.

Finally she said, "I do believe he's got you pegged, Edric. He recognizes a jackass when he sees one."

Taking no offense, Edric's chuckle deepened into laughter. Glancing over in time to see Kerry's flaming face, he pointed out none too kindly, "Well, Kerry, I'd like to be a patient of Dr. Neal Freeman's, but it just hasn't worked out that way." He grinned. "She's more fond of treating animals than me. Not that I haven't tried. She's even accused me of being a goose, now a jackass, but for all that I'm as healthy as a—"

"As a horse," Neal interjected, shaking her head at his triteness.

Edric grinned and nodded. "I even offered her the use of my body so that she could study the human anatomy, but alas, she refused even that." His eyes twinkled. "What an opportunity!"

"I suppose next that you'll tell me that you and Neal are no more than business acquaintances." Kerry ground out the words, not appreciating Edric's joke at his expense and resenting the easy camaraderie of Neal and Edric.

Edric's eyes darkened, and they never wavered from Kerry's face, but he made no effort to answer. Rather, he lifted his mug to his lips and drank deeply. Finally he set the mug down and wiped the back of his hand across his mouth. "I'm not telling you anything," Edric softly enunciated. "You'll have to guess exactly what my relationship to Neal is." He glanced at Neal and saw the fire billowing in her eyes, and he smiled, swinging his face back in Kerry's direction. "But I'll tell you this, I certainly wish it were more than what it is."

Neal almost collapsed on the bench from relief. She didn't realize that she'd been holding her breath for fear of what Edric would reply. As the same time she found that she was becoming increasingly exasperated with both men.

Edric's smile only widened when he saw her consternation. "Neal and I go a long way back. And back then, I can tell you, it was certainly more than business." He wiped the condensation from the mug, not looking at either Neal or Kerry.

Neal laid her fork on her place, picked up her napkin, and wiped her hands. Incensed, she breathed deeply, not daring to look at Edric, hating to see the hurt in Kerry's face.

"I don't recall your ever having mentioned Edric," Kerry softly commented, his interest diverted from his food and centered fully on Neal and her response.

"Edric and I dated when we were younger," she returned dryly, wondering if he was going to expect her to start giving an account of herself to him.

"Yet you didn't tell me about him!"

"Maybe I wasn't that important." Edric hazarded the guess, his eyes narrowed, warily studying Neal.

"Or maybe you were *too* important," Kerry countered coldly. "Too important for Neal to want to talk about."

Again Edric retorted, "She was that important to me, but who knows about Neal?" He smiled, deliberately adding, "Usually one doesn't forget his or her first love, but you can never tell about these modern, emancipated women. Maybe one love is that much like the next. Maybe no romance means too much to them."

Furious with both men, Neal looked from one to the other. Then she addressed Kerry in blistering tones. "No, I didn't tell you about Edric. Why should I? He was a memory from my past, and I wasn't ready to share him with you. He was my first serious boyfriend." Her voice was quiet, but Kerry and Edric could tell she was holding her anger in check. "Have you told me about all your old girl friends?" She shook her head. "I think not! Yet you get uptight over my puppy love!"

Edric's short laugh was ragged and dry. "Neal, I love your explaining me away to nothing. Here I sit, living and breathing, clearly one of those who is alive and well, yet you totally erase me from the face of the earth." He waved his hand. "Poof! There goes Edric Cameron. I'm beginning to wonder if I am one of your patients. I'm beginning to wonder who I am. What am I?" he demanded. "A goose, a jackass, a horse, a puppy, a vague memory from your past?"

At that moment Kerry wished that Edric were no more than a memory. He could accept that; he could handle that. Perhaps he could, in time, obliterate it, but he knew that he stood no chance against Edric Cameron, the man who was presently in Neal's life. He'd seen the way the two of them looked at each other. He'd felt the tenseness that their proximity generated for them. Without Neal's telling him, he knew that she wouldn't be marrying him, and he knew that she wouldn't be leaving Kerrville. Still, Kerry thought, he wouldn't give her up without a fight. He wouldn't make it easy for Edric to get her.

"No, Edric, you're not just a vague memory from her past," Kerry said. "I think you're very much a part of her present."

Neal could feel things slipping out of her hands. She was no longer in control of her own destiny. It seemed as if Kerry and Edric were tossing her fate back and forth between them like a ball. They were discussing her, talking about her as if she weren't present.

And the more she thought about it, the angrier she became with both of them. She cloaked her anger, however, and fought the tension that tied her stomach into knots. Gingerly she lifted her hand and massaged the base of her neck, hoping to release some of her stress.

"You're right, Kerry," she managed to assert, tossing her head proudly, looking him squarely in the eyes, meeting the challenge which he had issued. "Edric is very much a part of my present." She glanced over to see the gloating smirk on Edric's face. "He's the client, and I'm the veterinarian." Her words were clipped, precise, and brittle.

"You're just like Edric," she said, seething. "Given the chance you'd run my life, too." She ignored Kerry's shake of denial, her words running into heated thoughts. You'd dictate my life for me also. Well, neither one of you is going to do it, she decided. Just I, Neal Freeman, will make my decisions and choices.

Taking a deep breath, stifling the urge to walk away from both of them, Neal continued to speak in that faraway voice. "Remember I came here because I wanted a chance to do the kind of work that Sam does. I didn't want to be tied down to a clinic, treating house pets the rest of my life."

She spared Edric a glance and saw his brow furrowed and his eyes full of question. She knew without asking what he was wondering. He wanted to know why she was minimizing their relationship. Well, Mr. Cameron, she thought, keep wondering. It wasn't that she was ashamed of what she and he had shared, but she was ashamed of his behavior. She resented his butting into her affairs; she highly resented his putting her into this compromising situation, forcing her to explain more to Kerry than should have been necessary. She was also disappointed because he didn't trust her enough to let her tell Kerry by herself.

Edric wondered what she was thinking, and he wondered if perhaps his coming had been a mistake. What if his plan went awry? What if it backfired? And on second thought, he decided, maybe she did want the security that Kerry offered. Like her, though, he hooded his eyes with those thick sable lashes, keeping his thoughts, his questions, and his doubts to himself, presenting a bland, impassive face to both Neal and Kerry.

Reaching across the table, he picked up a small loaf of

bread that rested under the red and white checkered linen square in the basket. After breaking off the end crust and picking up Neal's knife, he buttered it. "You don't mind if I munch on this, do you?" he asked of neither one in particular. "I'm starved. Been in meetings all day, and I haven't had a bite to eat. Besides," he added, looking into those familiar blue eyes with the purple highlights, "I've had a lot on my mind. Been kinda worried about my favorite cat."

"Oh?" Kerry questioned, lifting his brows skeptically. Was this another one of Cameron's jokes? he wondered.

Neal lowered her head and simmered angrily. Her only retort, however, was: "An African cat, Kerry, not a house cat."

"Wrong, doc," Edric softly corrected, his face suddenly gone serious. "It's not an African cat. It's an American, one far more exotic than the African variety."

Neal slowly raised her face and looked into those eyes. "What's wrong with it?" she asked as softly, forgetting Kerry, forgetting everything else but her and Edric.

"I think she's got a hankering to leave the safety of the sanctuary." He paused. "I don't know if she's gonna make it out here or not."

There was a long, ponderous silence before Kerry finally cleared his throat and spoke. "And what will you do if this"—he paused, skepticism clearly stamped on his face—"if this—uh—cat of yours doesn't make it?" He looked back and forth from Edric to Neal.

Edric's eyes never left Neal's face. He smiled wistfully. "I've done all I can. Guess I'll have to turn her loose if that's what she wants."

"Would you?" Kerry asked, small sparks of interest splintering through his eyes.

Edric nodded his head. "If I have to."

"You may have to." Neal concurred quietly, dropping

her eyes, running her index finger over the design in the tablecloth Without lifting her face, she spoke, breaking the intimacy of the moment. "I don't mean to sound inhospitable, but Kerry and I haven't seen each other in several months, and we would like to have this evening to ourselves. We have personal things which we wish to discuss." Now she lifted her face and smiled. "Would you mind leaving us?"

Edric knew the moment was over. He nodded and smiled. Then he threw one last bite of bread into his mouth and chased it down with a swig of beer. "I'm sorry, Neal. I shouldn't have barged in on your date." He lifted his arm and looked at his watch. "I would have thought that Sam and Livy would be here by now. I'll wait for a few more minutes, and if they don't show up, I'll just mosey along." He looked at Neal, presenting a picture of innocence. "If that's all right with you?"

At the moment Neal opened her mouth to tell him that it wasn't all right, she was paged.

"Dr. Neal Freeman. Telephone call in the lobby."

Kerry grimaced. First Edric, now her job. "Are you on duty?" he asked as Neal looked around in surprise.

"That's one of the things you'll have to put up with," Edric said, watching Neal curtly nod her head in Kerry's direction. "Remember, last weekend, angel," he went on as she slid her chair back with the weight of her body, "when you and I were going to have dinner together at the Golden Corral."

The public address system blared out again "Dr. Neal Freeman. Please come to the lobby."

"Better get a move on," Edric enjoined briskly, raising his brows and nodding his head in the direction of the lobby. He noticed her glare, and her mouth was opened as if she were intending to make some kind of retort, but Edric wouldn't let her. He swung his gaze back to Kerry and continued talking as if he'd never been interrupted. "We had no more than finished our cocktails when the phone rang, and we spent the entire evening delivering Andrew Jordan's foal. Didn't get home until the wee hours of the morning." He grinned. "Our supper turned out to be breakfast, and what a breakfast!"

Neal spun around on her heels, marching to the lobby. She was so angry she could hardly see, so angry that she wanted to lash out. At the same time her heart felt like lead weighting her body down, and her eyes were dry and gritty. Edric had done his worst, and he'd done it well. No need to worry about what else he might say. He'd left little to Kerry's imagination.

"Dr. Freeman," she murmured to the young man behind the cashier's cage.

"Ah, yes, Dr. Freeman," he replied, a warm smile creasing his face. He pointed. "Right over there."

In a daze Neal moved to the phone and picked up the receiver. "Neal Freeman."

"Neal. Sam here. Just calling to let you know that Livy and I aren't waiting until morning to pull out. We're leaving tonight with the Parkers."

Neal blinked several times as Sam outlined his plans for her, and she tried to clear her mind. Finally she said, "I thought you were coming to the Bucking Bronc for supper?"

Sam laughed. "I don't know who gave you that idea, but I can guess." Then he guffawed as if it were some kind of hilarious joke. "But, no," he eventually said when he'd sobered up, "we're not coming to the Bucking Bronc this Friday evening. We're hitting the road as soon as Betty and Vince get here."

After a few more instructions and last-minute good-byes, Sam hung up, and Neal moved, trancelike, back to her table. Surprisingly though, she no longer felt angry;

she felt nothing but a horrible disappointment. She couldn't believe that Edric would stoop to such levels deliberately to mess things up for her. His exaggerations were more deceitful than outright lies; his presence had been an infringement on her evening. Unlike Edric, she didn't believe the end justified the means.

She lifted her leg and swung it over the bench. "That was Sam," she announced in a dry monotone, her eyes level with Edric's. "He and Livy are leaving for Yoakum tonight. They're driving down with the Parkers."

Edric searched her face, but other than the hurt and disillusionment that shadowed the purple irises, he saw no emotion.

"Said to tell you that they wouldn't be able to meet you for supper after all," Neal continued in the same bland tones.

Slowly Edric nodded his head. He understood exactly what Neal was saying. He'd taken a chance, and it'd backfired. The game was up, he guessed. He stood, motioning for the waiter.

"Well, folks, I'll be shoving off. Let you get back to your dinner and your conversation." He turned to the waiter. "Check, please, for the beer." Without waiting for him to figure it up, Edric pulled several bills from his wallet and handed them to him. "This should more than cover it, and you can keep the change." He turned his attention back to Kerry. "How long are you planning to be in town?"

Now it was Kerry's turn to retaliate. "Depends," he said, turning to look at Neal. "It all depends."

Neal dropped her face, refusing to be used by either one of them. She refused to submit to the pleading blue eyes that turned in her direction, and she refused to encounter the sardonic golden brown ones. She was angry that Edric had pushed Kerry into a corner, and she was embarrassed and hurt that he had pushed her into a premature confrontation with Kerry. Why hadn't he trusted her enough to handle the situation herself? Why hadn't he let her make her own decisions without trying to impose his will on her?

"Depends on what?" Edric relentlessly prodded, not caring what happened now, fighting for what he wanted most out of life—Neal.

"I've asked Neal to marry me," Kerry told him, clearly staking his territory, daring Edric to step across the line. "I want her to return to Beaumont with me. I've offered to buy into a clinic for her."

"Are congratulations in order?" Edric asked, barely disguising the anger and the simultaneous fear that thundered through his body, that pounded through his bloodstream.

"Not yet," Kerry answered quietly, projecting a confidence he was far from feeling. "She's going to give me her answer tonight."

An enigmatic smile hovered on Edric's lips. "I see," he murmured, placing his hands on his hips, staring at both of them for a second. His mouth opened as if he were going to speak again, but he just shook his head instead. Finally he turned his back to them and began threading his way through the tables.

Why not say it? he thought, stopping, looking over his shoulder. Why not make that one last all-out effort? He spun around and quickly retraced his steps. His smile was a bitter curving of the mouth and a reflection of his anxiety. When he spoke her name, both Neal and Kerry looked up at him in surprise, Neal's eyes wide with apprehension.

"When you get home tonight, will you check to see if I left my razor there last weekend? I seem to have misplaced it." He shrugged offhandedly. "I had to buy a new

165

one when I arrived in San Antonio, but it's not like my old one."

Neal's face blanched, and Kerry's contorted with anger. Edric's fingers feathered the tip of his hat, and he jauntily waved his departure, turning and confidently sauntering out the door.

CHAPTER EIGHT

Neal stood at the window of the old ranch house on the Golden Cam with her back to Edric. "No, Edric," she said in answer to his question, "I'm not going to marry Kerry, and, no," she further elucidated, "I didn't have to sleep with him last weekend before I made my decision." Her voice was dull and monotonous, lacking any type of animation. Wearily she raked her hands through her curls, gently massaging her temples.

She heard Edric's movement behind her, and she turned to see the relief that flooded his countenance, but it meant little to her. Dispassionately she watched the small tug of his lips that turned into a full smile; she saw the twinkle return to his eyes. Yet none of it touched her.

Edric, however, didn't notice her lackluster eyes. He was so happy that she hadn't slept with Kerry and that she wasn't returning to Beaumont that he deliberately overlooked the dullness in her voice. He threw his hat on the sofa and walked to her; his hands clasped her shoulders.

"I knew you couldn't marry him. I just knew you couldn't." He pulled her to him and rained quick, fiery kisses over her face, still unaware of her lack of response. "I knew you couldn't return to Beaumont. You came back to Kerrville because of what we'd had together, and you couldn't leave."

Neal quickly disentangled herself from Edric's grasp

167

and walked farther into the room, not stopping until she stood in front of the large table. "That's just it, Edric," she replied deadpan, "I am leaving."

She heard the crisp thud of Edric's boots as he moved across the hardwood floor, coming to stand in front of her. "You're leaving!" It wasn't a question. It was a ghastly cry from his soul. "Oh, no!" he vehemently enjoined with authority. "You're not leaving."

"And how do you propose to stop me?" she asked in that same deathly quiet voice.

Edric didn't reply immediately. He just continued to stare at her. Then it was as if something had snapped inside him. He had to bow to the inevitable. "I'll think of something," he muttered defiantly.

He lowered his face and began to unsnap the cuffs of his shirt and to roll them up, exposing his sinewy forearms, flexing the muscled wrist and hands that were covered with that shadow of fine hair. Neal became a part of the aura of inevitability that each of his movements generated. She was fixed to her position, her eyes never leaving his hands. Yet all the while she seemed to be more a spectator than a participator.

"I've already told Sam," she said. "I told him that I wouldn't be buying into his practice."

Edric stepped closer to her. He lifted one of his large hands, balled it into a fist, gently tapped her chin, and forced her to look into his eyes. For a long time and with a searching intensity, his eyes explored the caverns of her soul. He desperately tried to find her in the complicated maze. Finally he leaned forward; his lips softly touched hers.

Impassively Neal stood, letting him touch her but never responding. Edric pulled back. "What's the matter, honey?" he said, taunting her gently. "Afraid it'll resurrect some pleasant memories?"

Neal shook her head. "No, I'm not afraid of that. Quite the reverse, in fact."

Edric's eyes narrowed. "Afraid that I'll conjure up bad ones?" he gibed harshly. "Or better yet, afraid that I'll contaminate your memories?"

"I'm not afraid that you'll conjure up bad memories or that you'll contaminate the ones that I have," Neal explained. "All my memories are safely locked away, and no one, not even you, can reach them." She twisted her head, freeing herself from his hand. As much as she would have liked to be immune to his touch, she wasn't.

"I don't want to contaminate them, love," he softly said, moving closer to her. "I want to add more to them. I want to give you new memories, better memories." When he finished speaking, his lips feathered across hers again. "Like this," he murmured, his lips traveling to the slender column of her neck. "Or like this." His lips still moved, lightly kissing her neck up to her ears.

Neal's body wanted to listen to the impassioned cries of Edric's arousal; it wanted to turn traitor to her commands. But she refused to capitulate. She stood firmly on her resolution. "This isn't the answer," she gently told him. "At most we'll make love, but it will have solved none of our differences."

He didn't listen. His strong arms caught her tightly to him, and again his lips tried to capture hers, but she twisted in his arms and flailed. He caught her errant, pounding hand in one of his and pulled it behind her back, his lips now free to travel the arched curve of her collarbone, lower to the soft swell that was revealed by the V of her shirt.

"You're stronger than I am," she panted, twisting from side to side in his arms, "and eventually I'll become a willing partner, but after we make love, Edric, where will we be? What will we have accomplished?"

"Everything," Edric whispered, his lips moving over her face, her lips, her eyes, her cheeks, back to her mouth. "You want me as much as I want you. You need me as much as I need you. We're made for each other, Neal."

Need! Need! Need! The words whirled through Neal's mind, getting louder and louder by the second, pulsating painfully through her brain. That's all it was to Edric— plain and simple. It was need and want. Nothing more than a physical coming together of two bodies. All his talk about soul affinity had just been a sham, talk and nothing more. If she stayed, if she did agree to an affair, she knew it would be one based on a mutual need and want, not one based on love, trust, or respect.

Giving one hard shove, Neal extricated herself from his arms and glared at him. "If I hadn't known your mother better and if I hadn't respected her, I'd call you a classic son of a bitch." Her eyes filled with tears of anger and remorse for what could have been, for what had been destroyed. "Twice in my life I've let you drag me through hell. The first time I would have willingly accepted that and asked for nothing better. This time I *refuse* to stay down here with you." When he took a step toward her, she moved backward, shaking her head. "I trusted you, Edric Cameron, and look what you've done to me. You betrayed me."

Edric shook his head. "Don't try to tell me that you don't want me." He challenged her in a flinty voice. "You're a little too late for that."

"Are 'want' and 'need' the only two words in your vocabulary?" Neal demanded quietly. "Have you never thought about trust or respect?" Although two tears slowly rolled down her cheeks, she began to laugh. "My telling you that I loved you didn't mean a thing to you, did it? All you could think about was a sure guarantee for your pleasure. It didn't matter that you humiliated me in front of Kerry as long as Edric Cameron got what he wanted. And right then he wanted Neal Freeman, and right now he wants Neal Freeman." As she spoke, she moved away from him.

Picking up her hat from the sofa, flipping it on her head, she walked to the door. "Perhaps your coming to the Bucking Bronc the other night was good thing after all, Edric. I learned something." She stopped talking, her hand resting against the screen door, but she didn't shove. "I don't want you. I simply don't want you, and I don't need you." She smiled. "I learned that you're a dishonest man and a dishonest lover who'll use any means available to get what you want. I'll have to concede, though," she said magnanimously, "that you make sure you give pleasure in return, but deep down, Edric, you don't care. You never cared for me, Neal, the woman, the person underneath. You never tried to discover the soul of me. You couldn't accept that I needed time before I accepted our relationship on your terms, so you chose to trick me into continuing without letting *me* choose what I wanted myself. You didn't give me the chance to accept or to refuse."

"Neal," Edric began, "please give me a chance—"

"I hope you're satisfied," she continued, giving no heed to his plea. "Kerry left believing that we were lovers, living together, thinking the worst of me. But that's what you wanted, wasn't it? You weren't even willing to trust me to break up with him, were you?"

Again Edric opened his mouth to say something, but the words wouldn't come. They seemed to be stuck in his throat, lumped together. Finally he breathed deeply and pushed his fingers through his hair.

Neal spoke again, her voice soft and gentle this time. "I came home, Edric, to find you. And I fell in love with you again, or rather, I fell in love with the man I wanted you to be, the man who would complement my life. I wanted

171

a lover who would be tender and gentle, who would be loving and warm, who would be giving. Who would be part of me. But this is all just talk to you, Edric. You're basically a coward, frightened by the unhappy shadows of your past, afraid to catch hold of today and to take a chance on tomorrow. You're afraid, and your fear makes you cold and hard, grasping and greedy."

Neal stared at Edric's ashen face for a second, and she almost ran to him. She wanted to comfort him, to wipe the hurt and anguish from his countenance. But she couldn't. If she were to give in now, she would gain nothing but a new heartache. In the end neither of them would win. As Neal saw it, she would lose either way she went.

"You can live your life without commitment if you want to," she said in a gentler tone, "but I can't, Edric, nor do I want to." Again she tried to laugh. "Funny thing, I'd given up the idea of looking for a ring from you. I didn't even expect marriage. I was going to accept whatever you offered, whatever you wanted. All I asked in return was an 'I trust you, Neal,' or an 'I love you, Neal.' But even that was too much, wasn't it?" She looked at him with painful accusation. "You're really an empty person, Edric." She pushed the screen door open. "I just wanted to come by to tell you good-bye. And I wanted to wish you well in the future. I hope you find what you're looking for." She turned, walking away from him.

Edric stumbled to the couch and sank into its softness. As the front door slammed behind Neal, he began to feel the horrible constrictions of that acute loneliness that had gripped him first when his mother had died, next when his father had died. Now Neal had walked out on him. He was absolutely, totally alone. There was no one in his life who cared, who loved him.

Finally he walked to the window and stared across the lawn, watching the deer play. He remembered the day he

172

and Neal had stood here together, watching the deer and the horses. He wanted to show her. . . . He wanted to share it with her. . . . But she wasn't here. And he couldn't tell her about the grant. He couldn't share it with her.

Grief racked his body, and he stood still for a long time before he walked to the bar. When he moved to his bedroom, the room where he'd first made love to Neal, he carried one glass and a bottle of whiskey.

He didn't want to feel ever again.

CHAPTER NINE

It was hard for Neal to believe that summer was ending as she stared at the inviting coolness of the river that flowed behind the old ranch house. It was even harder for her to believe that it had been two months since she'd last seen Edric. But it had. After two weeks of constant calling and constant rejection Edric had given up. Slowly the past six weeks had crawled by, and each day Neal had found it harder and harder to stay away from him. She had no desire to live.

Gone were her dreams of yesterday, replaced with the pain and anguish of an old wound that was gaping open again. Still, she couldn't leave Kerrville without coming back to the old place one more time. She knew that she was leaving this time for good, and she wouldn't be returning. The decision to leave had been relatively easy, almost painless. If only she could get rid of the memories that easily, she thought. Maybe in time, she hoped.

She lay on a thick tuft of grass, cradling her head in her hands, listening to the lazy summer sounds around her. Hidden beneath the drooping boughs of the willow, she let her thoughts slide into that hazy region that was somewhere between dozing and sleeping, the warm green foliage of the trees imprinted on her mind. Her mother had always called them weeping willows, she thought. If that were true, then she and the willow were one. Both of them wept. She wept over her lost love, and she wondered why the willow wept. Had the tree lost its lover, too? Had it been swept down the river during one of the raging floods? Poor tree, she murmured, falling into a light sleep.

It wasn't until she felt the soft, whispery movement on her lips that she lethargically lifted her heavy, slumberous lids. She saw Edric leaning over her, twitching a blade of grass over her upper lip.

"Edric," she whispered, still more asleep than awake, "what are you doing here?"

"I'm waking Sleeping Beauty," he returned softly, not daring to break the sweetness of the moment, yet willing her to awaken. "It seems to be one of the duties in my life where you're concerned."

Neal smiled, rubbing her hand across her mouth. Then she rolled over and pushed herself into a sitting position, brushing her fingers through her tangled curls. "Sorry," she said, "I guess I did fall asleep."

Edric smiled slowly, a lazy lifting of his mouth. "Sound asleep." He held the blade of grass up. "You ought to be proud of me. I didn't take advantage of your sleeping to kiss you awake."

Yet his words were as strong as a physical caress; they were like a kiss. She could taste the sweetness of his kisses. She could feel the softness of his mouth moving on hers, warm, moist, questing. She couldn't trust herself to speak, so she just nodded.

"How come you're out this way?"

Neal shrugged. "I came to tell Molly good-bye."

"You're leaving?"

Neal nodded, mutely staring down at her hands that were clasped together in front of her. Then she averted her face, staring at the river rather than at Edric. She didn't want to go; she wanted to stay here with him. And if he began to persuade her, she knew she had no resistance. Still, she had to fight him to retain her integrity.

"I'm on my way now."

"Where are you going?"

Neal plucked a blade of grass and pulled it through her fingers. "Newton first to see Mom and Dad." She tilted her face to the side and looked curiously at him. "How'd you know that I was here? Molly call you?"

Edric nodded, rolling over on his back, staring up through the heavy foliage of the trees. "*Umhum,*" he droned contentedly, adding no more. He just closed his eyes.

Neal squirmed so that she could look at him, and she noticed a difference. It wasn't just the clothes, she decided, wondering why he was dressed in slacks and a sport shirt. It was something else. He didn't seem to be so arrogant or jaunty. He seemed humbled somehow, a man with an air of defeated resignation about him. He seemed to be passively accepting her decision to leave.

"Why were you leaving without seeing me?" he asked.

Was she? she wondered. Probably not.

"I was leaving as soon as I'd come back to the river," she said evasively, looking at the calm water that reflected the brilliant hues of the noonday sun. "I love this place, and I couldn't leave without coming back one more time." She laughed gently. "I sneak up here all the time."

"You haven't sneaked up here in over two months," Edric said accusingly, softly, still not moving his head, not opening his eyes.

"How do you know?" Her voice sounded lighter, happier.

Now he did turn his head, and he stared into her face. "Because I've been up here most of the time. I've lived here since you walked out on me." She saw the dull,

176

throbbing pain in his eyes. "Why wouldn't you talk to me when I called, Neal? Why didn't you return my calls?"

Neal shrugged, unable to tear her eyes away from his. "There was no need, Edric. You think like you do, and I think like I do. I don't think we're really compatible. We're worlds apart."

Edric pulled a face of indifference. "Maybe you're right," he said, offering no argument. Then, with sudden, lithe movements, he sat up. "I'm hungry. Care to have lunch with me?"

Neal turned her arm and looked at her watch. "I need to get started."

Again Edric didn't push her. Again he moved cautiously. "Up to you," he said casually, sprinting to his feet. "I'm going to fix me something. Come along if you wish."

He moved toward the house, and Neal sat for the longest while, watching him. When he walked up on the porch, he pulled on the screen door and turned to stare at her. Yet he said nothing. In the second that their eyes locked, Neal jumped to her feet, brushing the twigs from her jeans, and she ran across the lawn, up the steps, preceding him into the kitchen.

"What are you fixing?" she asked as he opened the refrigerator door.

He pulled out packages of luncheon meats and cheeses, putting them on the counter. Next he found the lettuce and tomatoes, the pickles, the mustard, the mayonnaise. A pot of beans followed. Still he rummaged for more. "Here's some cold roast beef," he announced, "and here's some of Molly's apple pie."

"What a spread!" Neal said. "What are you going to have?" She walked to the sink and washed, then grabbed for the paper towels. As she dried her hands, she moved to the table and stood across from him.

Edric straightened and looked at her. Then his large

hand reached out, and he gently pushed his fingers through the tousled curls. "I like it all," he said, shrugging his shoulders, his fingers lightly wisping over the pearly skin. He smiled. "I'll have whatever you want." A world of meaning was in his words.

Neal swallowed, understanding the double meaning. Again she wiped her hands on the paper towel, but this time it wasn't water she was drying off them. It was the perspiration of anticipation and the apprehension. She smiled, letting her eyes light up, letting the sunshine of her happiness filter through.

"How about a roast beef sandwich?"

Edric nodded. "Sounds fine to me."

"Or better yet," Neal said, "we'll fix all of it, so we can have a little bit of each. That way we'll get to taste all of it."

He nodded. "If that's what you want." Again he said no more.

Shattered by the sensuous shine of his eyes and the caressive strains of his voice, Neal returned quietly, "It— it sounds like a good idea to me." Her eyes responded to his, telling him in silent but eloquent language that there was still a thread of hope—but just a thread.

"Neal," Edric said, moving around the table, his mind definitely not on food, "I want to talk to you. There's so much I have to say." He hesitated before adding on a lowered note, "To explain to you."

Neal moved away from his closeness. "Not right now," she replied, making a show of reluctance. For the first time she was in command, and for the moment she wanted Edric to remain uncertain about her eventual decision. "Let's eat first. Then we'll talk. Okay?"

Again he stared at her before he reluctantly nodded. Though arrogant denial momentarily blazed in his eyes, he quickly squelched it and followed her lead. Through the meal Neal managed to keep up a light and easy conversation, but once they had finished and once the dishes were washed and dried, Edric caught her hands and dragged her into the living room. "Now we talk," he declared with an emphatic softness.

Neal knew that something momentous was about to happen to both of them, something that would change the present course which she had plotted for her life. Her breathing quickened with hope that Edric was ready to make a commitment of love and trust to her. It was the only thought that kept her level-headed.

"Would you like another cup of coffee," Neal asked prosaically, as if she were the hostess and Edric were the visitor.

"No, thank you, Neal," Edric returned softly. "I don't think coffee is what either of us wants right now." His golden brown eyes flamed with the fire of his desire.

Again, however, the word "want" diminished Neal's pleasure and kept her from retorting with the light "And what do you want?" Although his use of the word doused the hope that had been flaring in her heart, she continued to look at him, her entire being questioning him, wondering what the outcome of this confrontation would be.

He reached out and caught both her hands in his and held them, not attempting to pull her closer, just standing there, looking at her, drinking in her beauty, tasting the love that radiated from her whether she wanted it to or not, whether she was aware of it or not.

"I want to talk first," he replied to her silent inquisition. "There's a lot I need to say, a lot I need to apologize for."

Neal's body almost collapsed with his words, and her blood began to race through every cell in her body, revitalizing her. Hope, resurrected, began to sing the song of new birth. Her legs were weak and wobbly; she could hardly stand. Her breathing was more shallow than before, and heartbeat accelerated so that she could hardly hear Edric over the roar in her ears. In spite of her resolution to stand firm, not to capitulate, she found herself wanting to lean against him. She wanted to be held in those strong arms, to be kissed by those firm, sensuous lips. Now it was she who wanted!

"I missed you, darling," he whispered. "And these past few weeks were worse than hell for me." He raised his hand, letting his fingertips trace the smooth line of her jaw, the length of her nose, the curve of her full lips. His eyes followed the path that his fingers blazed. "You've turned my world upside down," he confessed, but this time there was no anguish in his words, no pain in the confession. "You've given me cause to reevaluate everything I've stood for and thought I believed in."

Although Neal could easily have drowned in the pools of love that bubbled invitingly in Edric's eyes, although she wanted to throw herself into his arms, to be kissed senseless, to be loved, she stood holding herself rigid.

"And what conclusion did you come to?" she asked in a faintly husky voice.

"I'm sorry that I didn't trust you, Neal," he drawled, "but believe it or not, I cared too much this time, and I was afraid of losing you again. I knew how much you wanted marriage, a family, security, all the things that I wouldn't offer to you."

"You really care?" Neal questioned tremulously, wonderingly, the words sounding so beautiful, so fulfilling.

"I do," he affirmed emphatically. "I found out that I'm no longer afraid of the past, Neal. It's over and done with, but I also discovered that I'm afraid of the future without you."

Somehow they were tangled in each other's arms, and Neal was rubbing her cheeks against his chest, her arms drawing him closer and closer. She lifted her face, begging for his touch; then his lips captured hers in a long soul-searching kiss. As he held her, as his lips moved over hers, her fingers began to unsnap the front of his shirt and to slip inside to rub against the furry mat of hair.

"But, baby," he whispered, his lips lifting from hers, moving to the silken tendrils that covered her ears, "I also found out that I need and want you. I know that rubs you the wrong way, but I want you, Neal. I need you." He drew a sharp, ragged breath. "Not just for a day or a night, sweetheart. Not for just a weekend. But I want you by my side for the rest of my life. I want you to be my wife, to share my life. And I want us to have a houseful of kids who in turn will give us a houseful of grandkids—"

"Wait a minute," Neal shrieked. "I don't want to be the old woman in the shoe."

"Oh, well," he conceded easily. "Half a house then. As long as we make love like we plan to populate the entire world."

"*Umm,*" Neal murmured, "I like that idea."

She pulled his shirt off his shoulders, letting it drop negligently at their feet, and his searching fingers moved inside her shirt, deftly undoing the front, slipping it aside. His hand cupped her breast, his mouth moving downward, feathering fiery kisses over the exposed swell above her lacy bra.

Groaning her submission, forgetting their differences, Neal lifted her arms, closing them around his body, her fingers digging into the tensed muscles of his back, her face burrowing into the softness of the hair on his chest. Then she lifted her face and met his questing lips, snuggling closer, pressing herself against him as the thrust of his tongue filled her mouth.

When Edric finally lifted his lips, Neal's hands were tangled in his hair, and she was breathless and flushed with excitement. "What made you change your mind?" she asked, her voice ragged with her desire.

"You," he whispered. "Just you." His eyes hungrily devoured her, his hands running up and down her spine, sending molten passion spilling through her body. "I missed you," he confessed quietly. "That's all, sweetheart. I missed you. Without you there was no joy in my life. I had no one to share with, no one to laugh with, no one to love with, no one to grieve with." Suddenly his arms tightened around her, and she felt the desperation that racked his body. "I was alone, Neal, all alone. And I knew then that it was more than sex. I—"

He hesitated, and Neal felt pain as it shafted through her heart. She tried not to think about the possibility of Edric's having slept with someone else.

"I could have found sex with any woman, Neal. But I found that I didn't want just sex. No one appealed to me. All my want, all my needing were wrapped up in you, and you were gone. A part of me had been ripped away, and I was standing there with a gaping sore that wouldn't heal."

Neal found herself voicing her doubts. "Did you—did you—" She wanted to ask the same question which she'd condemned Edric for asking.

He lifted a finger and placed it gently across her lips, shushing her, shaking his head all the time. "No, darling, I didn't. That's when I knew that you were wrong." When she lifted her eyebrows, he explained. "You accused me of wanting and needing you. Superficial, you said, nothing more than sex. When I realized that I didn't want another woman, that another woman wouldn't do, I realized that in my heart I loved you. I just camouflaged it with other words. I was afraid to commit myself, so I used words which I thought were noncommittal." He laughed, his joy bubbling over. "But all the time I was committed to you, sweetheart. Like you said, love makes the commitments; love honors the demands."

Neal's hands twined behind his neck, and she looked at him with all her love beaming in her face, causing her eyes to glow, causing her cheeks to sparkle with blushing color. Her lips curved into a radiant smile, and they begged for his touch. And like all people in love, she wanted to hear those very old but very special words.

"How much time we've wasted, my love, just because you've been too obstinate to recognize your feelings for me," she said teasingly.

He grinned. "Just like a woman," he said. "Blame it on the man."

Neal pulled back and glared up at him. "And I suppose you're going to say that it's my fault!"

Now he chuckled richly. "I never thought about a definition of love before," he confessed softly, "but if it means wanting us to share our lives, to explore and to discover together, to ask each other's advice and help—if that's love, my darling, then I'm madly in love. There's no ending to my love for you."

Tears of happiness glazed her eyes, and she could hardly speak. "It's taken you a long, long time to say those words, Edric Cameron."

The golden brown eyes were twinkling, and a soft smile played around the corners of his lips. "I really had this figured out some time ago," he retorted, "but a certain, stubborn young woman messed things up."

"Oh?"

"I knew it for sure the night you met Kerry, and I knew it the day you walked out on me."

"Why did you wait so long to tell me?" she demanded in the same arrogant and proprietary tones that she had resented in Edric not so long ago.

"Stubborn, I guess. When you walked out, I decided

that I wasn't going to change. I'd lived this long without commitments, so why change now?" He grinned mischievously at her. "I wasn't going to buckle under to any woman. But I soon learned that without you, life held no interest for me. The women that I dated were dull and faceless to me; none of them excited me the way you did. Or touched me the way only you can—down to my very soul. Not one of them shared with me like you did."

"Oh, Edric," Neal cried, "we've wasted so much time. Why didn't you knock my door down to tell me?"

He shrugged and smiled sheepishly. "I'm really a coward at heart, darling. You were right about that. I wasn't sure what your feelings would be. I knew that whether I liked it or not, I was committed to you, but I was afraid that you'd changed your mind about me." After catching her shoulders and gently moving her aside, he walked across the room. "I stayed here at the old house in hopes that you'd come back. Day in, day out I waited." His face was grimly set with haunting memories. "I knew if you still cared that you'd come back, and I lived in hope of that day."

Neal licked her lips, which were dry. Her voice, when she spoke, was cracked and hoarse. "What if I hadn't come, Edric?"

He turned and looked into her face, smiling. "I was getting dressed to come to your place when Molly called to let me know that you were headed up to the house. So I lit out." He chuckled. "Not a chicken this time, sweetheart," he said in denial. "Just wise. I knew how proud you could be, and I didn't want the sight of my truck to discourage you from coming."

"Where—where've you been?" Neal asked.

"I drove around the bend, parked the truck at the check station, and walked back here to find you fast asleep under the willow tree." He picked his jacket up and fumbled through the pockets. When he found what he was search-ing for, he dropped the jacket and walked to Neal. With-out touching her, just looking at her ponderingly, he asked, "Neal, will you marry me?"

Tears coursed down her cheeks, and she mumbled her yes.

He opened the small box and took out an engagement ring. "Will you wear my ring?"

"Oh, Edric." She sobbed, taking the ring in one hand, wiping her cheeks with the other one. "It's beautiful. So beautiful."

"Here, clumsy," he said fondly, "let me put it on your hand." He lifted her left hand and slid the ring on the fourth finger. He smiled, but there was no levity in his tone. "I want the world to know that you're mine, Neal Freeman. I especially want the men to know."

Neal grinned, nodding her head, too full of happiness to do more than sniff her tears back and mutely acknowl-edge. Yet her feminine curiosity couldn't be quelled. "When did you buy it, Edric?"

"I bought it when I was in San Antonio," he said. "That's why I wanted you to come down that weekend. I planned to ask you to marry me, and I wanted to give you the ring." His golden brown eyes, warm and happy, reflected nothing but the image of her face. "Kerry threw a few kinks into my plans and almost drove me out of my mind."

"Oh, Edric," Neal cried again, "if only I'd known." She flung herself against him, wrapping her arms around him. "But you started acting so high-and-mighty, taking things into your hands, and you never really let me know that you cared."

He smiled tenderly. "I know, so maybe it's a good thing that we waited. Even if I had given you the ring in San Antonio, it would have been entirely because your kind of love demanded it, not because I had finally faced how much I love you. As it is, I now give you the ring and ask you to marry me because I want the same kind of commitment that you do."

"I love you, darling. I love you so very much."

Again Edric set Neal away from him and looked deeply into her eyes. "Neal, it's going to be touch and go for a long time. I've got the property, but I don't have much in the way of liquid assets."

"I don't care," Neal returned. "I've never been wealthy. I won't miss what I've never had."

He smiled, excitement welling up in his eyes. "I did get a government grant, though, so that means we won't be destitute, and we'll be working with several zoos. However," he said, his voice becoming quite serious and heavy, "there is one drawback to this grant." Neal's brow furrowed with anxiety; then Edric said, "I must hire a full-time veterinarian. Do you have any suggestions?"

Neal giggled, then pretended to think for a few seconds. "Well," she finally said, "I do happen to know a veterinarian who has just given up her job. If you can convince her that the advantages outweigh the disadvantages, she just might consider joining the Golden Cam."

Edric's hands closed over the large brass belt buckle at his waist, and he began to unfasten it. "Since I *truly* believe the advantages of the job far outweigh the disadvantages, I think I might be able to convince the veterinarian in question to accept my offer." He sat on the sofa and took off his boots and socks. Then he stood to unzip his slacks and step out of them.

All the time Neal's hands were busy unsnapping her shirt. "I've heard she's pretty stubborn. She might need a lot of convincing," she returned, shedding her clothes, letting them lie where they fell.

"I've got all the time in the world," he said, moving

186

toward her. His arms went around her slender, pliant body. "Shall we go into my office to discuss it?"

As they walked into the bedroom, Neal murmured, "I'm afraid it might take more than discussion, Mr. Cameron. This veterinarian is a hard person to convince."

"Dr. Freeman," he returned in a caressive whisper, "I'm a most patient man." At her burst of laughter he rephrased his statement. "In most cases I'm a most patient man. I'll expend all effort to convince this veterinarian of the advantages of remaining here on the Golden Cam as both the first lady and as the horse doctor. And I do have other means of persuasion besides just talking."

Neal giggled, falling onto the soft downy mattress. "Like I said, Edric Cameron, you're a gander, but I love you."

His last coherent words were: "I don't mind being your gander as long as you're my goose."

Then their laughter turned into soft sighs of pleasure. Finally their lips met in a kiss that was the melding of two souls in a binding union of love.

LOOK FOR NEXT MONTH'S
CANDLELIGHT ECSTASY ROMANCES ®

NEW DELL

CANDLELIGHT
Ecstasy Supreme

TEMPESTUOUS EDEN,
by Heather Graham.
$2.50

Blair Morgan—daughter of a powerful man, widow of a famous senator—sacrifices a world of wealth to work among the needy in the Central American jungle and meets Craig Taylor, a man she can deny nothing.

EMERALD FIRE,
by Barbara Andrews
$2.50

She was stranded on a deserted island with a handsome millionaire—what more could Kelly want? Love.

NEW DELL

CANDLELIGHT Ecstasy Supreme

LOVERS AND PRETENDERS,
by Prudence Martin
$2.50

Christine and Paul—looking for new lives on a cross-country jaunt, were bound by lies and a passion that grew more dangerously honest with each passing day. Would the truth destroy their love?

WARMED BY THE FIRE,
by Donna Kimel Vitek
$2.50

When malicious gossip forces Juliet to switch jobs from one television network to another, she swears an office romance will never threaten her career again—until she meets superstar anchorman Marc Tyner.

A woman's place—the parlor, not the concert stage! But radiant Diana Ballantyne, pianist extraordinaire, had one year before she would bow to her father's wishes, return to England and marry. She had given her word, yet the moment she met the brilliant Maestro, Baron Lukas von Korda, her fate was sealed. He touched her soul with music, kissed her lips with fire, filled her with unnameable desire. One minute warm and passionate, the next aloof, he mystified her, tantalized her. She longed for artistic triumph, ached for surrender, her passions ignited by Vienna dreams.

A DELL BOOK 19530-6 $3.50

Vienna Dreams

by JANETTE RADCLIFFE